Marita

just daniel freaker

© 1999 by Daniel Freaker

All rights reserved.
No part of this book may be reproduced or utilized in any form or by any means, electronic or mechanical, including photocopying and recording, or by any information storage and retrieval system, without written permission.

Printed by:
Imprenta Vistalegre
Phone +34 957 421 616
E-mail infovista@imprentavistalegre.com
Córdoba (Spain)

D.L. (Registration): CO-1.258/1999

I.S.B.N.: 84-88423-128

I would like to thank for support and, sometimes provocation, with a
subtlety and sympathy which I could not have presumed:
Elvira Pérez, for saying "yes";
Wendy Freaker, for pure acceptance;
Dorothea Maraki, for emotional comprehension;
Denis Masi, for the benefit of the doubt;
José Pérez, M.ª Teresa Vallejos, and José M.ª Pérez,
for uncommunicated support;
and those at Imprenta Vistalegre.

Homage to Albert Camus.

Dedicated to the memory of:

Ronald and Betty Freaker
Adi
Nunu
Ann
Osho

Chapter *1*

On his way to pay a visit to his grandmother, in order to satisfy a commitment, which he loathed having pledged, he paid little attention as to why he was going at all. He had said he would and knew that it would be remembered for a long time if he did not. Everything, all memories, were always catalogued, dated and filed, to be looked up and shared, to lend an emphasis to the argument at hand, excruciatingly out of context.

The relationship with his mother was absurd, it was something that they both accepted with inevitability, but it was far worse with his grandmother. No matter what hour of the day or what he was doing her image could pop into his mind just to remind him that there was someone about whom he should be thinking. A poor widow living on her own with little help from anyone. He had enormous trouble looking after himself, let alone never being able to go away on holiday or anything because someone had to feed the cat. He knew what was expected, but every time he tried to fulfil any expectations she would always manage to remind him that if he wanted gratitude then he would have to abide by her rules, obviously she knew best. Besides, she had been around much longer and lived through far worse.

Even without approval he still possessed an overpowering feeling that he was responsible, not that she felt that he was capable of being responsible for himself, but he was somehow responsible for her. Unable to walk past a nursing home without wondering when she might end up in one, two feelings came with this question: first, at least someone, however undeserving, would be able to look after her properly and a certain amount of weight would be taken off his shoulders. Secondly, the other perspective that he managed to conjure up by placing himself, hypothetically, in her position, was how awful it would be to spend what would probably be years, in her position, living like that; even though, theoretically, she would have company in a home the exposure from lack of privacy would probably make her feel more lonely. For the most part it was the loneliness that he was afraid of and he understood that thinking in this way, if disclosed, would seem selfish. His entire relationship with his grandmother, if he thought about it rationally, seemed to stem from a desire to be congratulated by her, however impossible it might be. The impossibility never quite became visible, perhaps it was obscured by his guilt for thinking so selfishly, but if it did then there would be little hope of it continuing.

Nobody wants to make an effort only to be mocked at the end of it; however humorously the mocking was implied. It was all right a few years before, when he was sixteen or seventeen, but he noticed that the older he became the more he was expected to do and the higher the content of malice in her comments. Before she would tell him what to do and he would do it as well as he could, but now he was expected to perform without notification. As he pursued this role he noticed how psychosomatically tired he would be shortly before he would make his scheduled, Sunday, phone call to her. Obviously, it would only take a minute and he would be enthusiastic afterwards, but he would make up any excuses not to, fully aware that it would make her feel like he did not care. He did and he might even more if he did not feel like she was making up excuses for him to care.

He found what she would call an ability to change her mind, but what he called an inability to make up her mind, extremely debilitating; her mind more often than not swung in a critical direction, giving all a terrible appearance, at which point he could not think of anything or anyone but her. He too was able to do this, performing like a child in a tantrum and dress it up in maturity, as though he had inherited it, but he was not able to manipulate others as well as she could, his mother for instance.

It was the first time he had ever driven on the motorway since he gained his driving license a few months before. It was a few days before Christmas and a great deal of traffic was on the road, but he felt unusually liberated, thinking that the other drivers all knew him and cared. Two years out of date techno-trance playing, almost blowing the speakers, in a car that originally belonged to an old lady that would only take it out to do the laundry or shopping and had to give it up because her age meant she had to re-sit the test, which she failed. None of the other drivers could hear, but he pretended they could and that they were paying attention, impressed, even if they could they would probably be annoyed. Was everyone annoyed by his generation, unidentified, although the population seemed to credit them with being far more disciplined than they were?

Why did Gran keep up the relationship? She did not like what he was doing, and thought he was rude and corrupted. And if he neglected to call her when she sent him some money, with enclosed specifications as to what he should spend it on, then she would remind him again what his duty was. Why did she ask him to do anything if she were only going to find it disagreeable and bring it up the next time she wanted to persuade him how he was neglecting her, and how bad off she was? Was this a rule for his entire generation of peers?

He felt as though her wanting him to care and her feeling that he must care were so confused as to be inseparable. He really wanted to do something for her of his own accord, but he became aware that everything he did was so exhausting that it seemed pointless. Didn't she want him to love and support her without a question of whether or not he "should" be doing what he was? Did it not defeat the object almost entirely? After all the notion was possible, but the reality was that the side of him that she never allowed herself to see would only have gained her disapproval, even more so than the one he was already presenting.

Now he was driving away from his girlfriend, Cherry, as fast as the car could go. Cherry was going to spend Christmas on her own. He hated himself because he knew he was to blame however hard he tried to pin it on his grandmother, but there was no way that Gran was going to put up with her, even thinking about trying to bring Cherry was difficult. But either Gran had to be alone or Cherry did and there was more chance of Cherry forgiving him. It was a terrible decision to make, but his Gran was alone all year round, so by continually asking for reassurance that it was all right for him to go from Cherry he had left. Hurtling down the chalk white landscape towards the low winter sun.

It was ridiculous that he didn't want to go yet he was driving as fast as he could, perhaps he thought that the faster he got there the sooner he would leave. Would hours or even minutes make any difference?

It was about three o'clock and he knew that Gran was going to be cross with him and would say that she had expected him at lunch time, that the dinner had been waiting for them and was now ruined. She spent hours cooking, there wasn't much else for her to do, and so she would use all the utensils in the kitchen; she had a utensil for every conceivable cooking procedure possible. All multicoloured and gadgety, left over from the postwar era, collected from magazines, advertised with profound captions, headlines presented in shattered outlines, promoting their multiple uses. Each time she used one she would wash it up regardless as to whether she might use it again. It seemed that she not only did this to keep herself busy for longer, but she was becoming forgetful. Speaking aloud about her every action as though directing herself around the kitchen. Asking herself where things were continually, although she had lived there for years and should at least be able to negotiate the cupboards without even thinking.

But there was something more to it, as though she knew it wasn't necessary. Nothing surprised her unless it was threatening her moral values; nothing was new, nothing exciting, little innocence; perhaps she was purposely forgetful and only pretending, negotiating the present as if it was new, regardless of the fact that it had all been done and that she would now never see a future.

He was so used to being ignorant of things, having his views changed and persuaded, more often than not by himself, that he was wrong, that things were different from what he thought they were. He was osmatic by nature, always trying to be like his peers, affected, terribly, by everything they said about him.

He felt he was what he was denied. Wanting to be a person that sits around in a shit hole with wallpaper hanging off, carpet barely visible, obscured by cigarette butts, ash and whatever else the residents brought in from the street. Thinking that if his parents didn't care then he could become whatever was inherently inside him. Perhaps he didn't want to be in a place that cared, perhaps he didn't want to care.

He and his friends had started stealing when they were ten, he'd take things by shoving them underneath his jumper and walking out, each time thinking how unbelievable it was that he wasn't caught. When he told his friends he would always exaggerate to impress them with what he had done, then give them what he'd taken just in case the story wasn't persuasive enough. After a while there weren't many stores that he hadn't been banned from because he had become a compulsive shoplifter, taking things he didn't have any need for, their only use being tools for arbitrary recognition.

He always envied what other people had; it had become a cult to ware cheap labelled clothes. He thought that maybe if he were to inherit his friends style he would have whatever it was that he didn't.

Bristol was a far cry from anything he had known before he visited his friend Sam; they were walking to his house from the coach station and a couple of teenagers decided that they wanted Sam's Chicago Bull's cap. As they walked past they just took it, the bigger of the two pushed Sam against a car and then into a shop window, then ran off laughing. From his point of view it looked like it was just an ordinary school play fight for Sam who made it look like he was taking it in his stride, not looking too scared and acting as though nothing had been damaged. Somehow Sam thought this would rectify the fact that he'd been beaten in front of the newcomer on the first day, acting as though it happened every day instead of being tough enough to kick the shit out of them. That was Sam's new plan, always a trick up the sleeve, always a slight distortion of the truth, always a new lie.

Something he too picked up, only partially from Sam, and found himself participating in more and more frequently, until he found that he no longer remembered what really happened.

He just stood there scared shitless watching Sam being pushed, trembling, paralysed although it wasn't even he being tortured. He watched Sam walking off afterwards, tidying himself up, tucking his shoe tongues into his trousers, innocently thinking that justice was, ultimately, going to be done, it was only friendly and Sam was going to get his hat back.

'They're from Saint Paul's,' said Sam.

'What's that?' he replied.

'The area next to where I live, it's the roughest.' That made Sam look even wickeder, moreover it made the event seem even greater and was something else he could attach to the story when he told it back in school.

The next time he visited stealing from shops was all but obsolete, the emergence of drug taking had made the shops seem a bit too far; in fact it had made them too lazy to go out at all, except at night when they had to go out and buy alcohol. They somehow managed to obtain dope from the local pub. Asking them inside and then going into the toilets to do the "deal", which was the most enjoyable part, other than that there was only getting faced and falling asleep in arbitrary places; waking up, starting smoking again before breakfast which consisted of a dirty dish, cocoa pops, and extra sugar which was put on for some strange reason, probably for luck.

Then when it was dark and they had all had a few bottles of cheap strong alcohol, the bottles of which were all collected in various bedrooms belonging to a groupie blond girl (always blond), who they were all staying with because she was sleeping with most of them except him. The bottles presented like trophies in a long line on the mantel, taking precedence over belongings of any real importance like aerosol deodorants or cheap stereos. They would go out making profound statements about how much more drunk they were than each other, arguing about it determinedly. Going out was called a mission and the idea was to steal as many car signs as possible. The higher the value of the car the better the sign, the value of which they were all educated on.

Jake, who had a long blond ponytail, which never came undone, may have been the shortest, but was probably the most respected because he could understand, at least pretended to, the "raga" language that was always rude and funny. Language which always accompanied the "happy-hardcore" mixed tapes that were playing in everyone's fucked houses, which had trippy posters from raves that no one had ever been to, but everyone reminisced about what a "full-on" time they had there and how many drugs, which had definitely been spiked with something far in excess of their budgets, they had taken.

Jake kicked a car's wing mirror, obviously trying to knock it off, but it swung around and smashed the passenger's window.

'Shit,' screamed Jake. Only drawing more attention to themselves.

They all ran, as fast as their dizzy heads could take them. Down dark alley ways, none of which he had followed before. Laughter, which was extremely debilitating at this moment of need and the sound of car signs ringing in their pockets, surrounding them all the way until they found somewhere that they could eat or get drugs.

They walked into a twenty-four-hour chippy and ordered large chips in pitta each. The few other lonely customers, all holding cans of beer they were consuming discreetly, were staring at them. Then Jake started laughing and pointing at Tom who had brought into the shop a Vauxhall sign attached to the entire front grate of a car. Grabbing his chips he ran out of the shop without paying, never letting go of the grate and it claimed pride position on his wall. That was until his house was searched under suspicion of narcotics and a whole wall full of car emblems were found and removed for evidence. Tom had been prosecuted for stealing fifteen cars and criminal damage of another thirty. The judge had mistaken Tom to be part of another gang that had always removed the sign after they went joyriding.

The last time he had visited Bristol he had ended up sniffing glue, usually in a room with the curtains always drawn and the light on. He didn't remember much, there wasn't much conversation. Somehow memories are easier to maintain when they consist of words that can be verified. There were a few of them around a table, all boys, hats pulled down low, pony tails falling out underneath. Skinny white topless bodies presenting themselves in the dim light, all slouched in their chairs, with minimum exertion.

There was a duckling on the round table walking, waddling, around the circumference. It attracted all attention possible from the present spectators whose eyes were blood shot, half open, not moving, but following, intently, with peripheral vision. Every now and then a giggle would emerge as it passed one of them, unable to find a way down and escape. Half the people were strangers who were an acquaintance of an acquaintance just stumbling in for a place to sleep at night, if it was night at all, or to find something of value. They would be lucky, there wasn't even any food in the cupboards, there was hardly even anywhere to sit, not even a clear bit of floor to rest on, although that didn't seem to bother many of them.

Nobody even noticed the pierced man, with a skin head and various undistinguishable tattoos, until the duckling stopped walking past. It took quite a while for any of them to became aware of an absence, but they did because it was their entertainment for the evening. Looking up as though something had disturbed him, something had broken the rhythmic mundanity of this evening that was making them feel content.

'The fucking thing spilt my spliff,' said the pierced man, gesturing towards the rizzla and spilt tobacco and a tiny bit of dope on the table. 'It fucked my mix!' his voice growing louder and his face growing creases.

'That's my fucking duck man,' said Jake.

'Yeah man, it doesn't know any better,' came another voice that had just woken up. At which point the punk opened his mouth wide and slowly inserted the duck into it.

'Shit, we haven't got any food,' said someone in the shadows, as though the circumstance had made them aware of sustenance. Then the shaking duckling's head was released from the angry lips that had enclosed around its neck. The pierced man proceeded to smile at it and give it a kiss on its beak and put it gently back on the table, assuming that it wasn't torturous for it to be on the table. The duck, shaking and barely able to stand, squirted a long streak of shit across the table covering the precious upset mix and landing square in the punk's crotch. The table with the duck on it went flying across the room when the pierced man stood up and chased after it. That night they could hear cursing and crashing all over the house. Every now and then the punk would poke his head under their chairs and in the cupboard, no one tried to intervene, not even saying anything. He couldn't quite remember if the guy killed it or not, but thought the ending was better that way.

Following his Gran's directions he pulled of the M27 unable to use the clutch properly, feeling as though everything was going incredibly slowly after the timeless speed of the motorway. He drove through the barren landscapes of the New Forest, the sun strobing through the trees made him want to shut his eyes and watch, to retreat with a reassuring presence. The scattered forests shared with arid landscapes of heather, gorse, often only present in black ash like skeleton form, and small lakes that had shores of flint shingle. The lakes seemed like puddles in comparison to when he had played around and in them when he was a child. And he realized why, when he was young, he didn't understand why they were called ponds; it made him smile, shortly. When he would go on expeditions to the ponds he used to wear the bright yellow Wellingtons his Gran had taken off her Paddington Teddy bear; the bear had seemed to be another resident of the house because it had been understood through comparison with himself. When you're young, how much bigger things are than you matters, and he couldn't say, during exhaustive arguments, that his daddy was bigger than theirs so they should watch out because he didn't have a father. Never did.

He had been forced to hear the repetitive announcements about how his mother had wanted a child and his father had agreed to her having, but didn't want to have anything to do with. So instead of emulating, in the supposed normal way, a figure of absolute security and strength such as the father figure, he would learn from Grandad's way of doing things, slowly, vulnerably and with dated methods. Following Grandad around obediently, wearing Grandad's fishing cap, ignorant of any kind of popular culture of the early eighties, juxtaposing a child's innocent features with an elderly sixties fashion.

The world was fifties and sixties during the seventies and eighties, he learned from the spectacular space race, always wanting to be an astronaut. But whenever asked what he wanted to be he would reply that it would be fun to be a garbage man. Fascinated by popular cartoon illustrated geology books instead of the emergence of the ZX-Spectrum and BBC home computers, and spared the popular horror films or any films or television for that matter. So his grandfather played an incredibly relevant role in his life, providing, in certain ways, a vulnerable personality. To be a man meant going for walks with a walking stick and resting every hundred yards or so, it meant doing things slowly and making shuffling noises when walking. It meant thinking about things well in advance, such as meals and outings. It meant never being too adventurous. Perhaps it also bestowed on him a greater instinct or common sense, as though he had done most things already. Moreover, it meant silence.

He and Gran ate the cauliflower-cheese that she ritually made for him every time he visited, either that or Souffle with a side order of frozen peas. She always forced him to finish every last scrap with brown sliced bread to mop the sauce up in the same way her husband. Always delicious.

After watching a bit of telly Gran would go to bed saying he could stay up if he wanted and watch a film or something. She chucked the newspaper at him which she had bought for the sole purpose of the television section. It felt strangely silent. There were no more continuous comments about the weather and the central heating.

'Why hasn't it come on yet?' she would say in an authoritarian voice, as though he should know. Then, putting her hand on the radiator, and in a voice very different as though replying to herself, regardless as to what he might have said, 'oh, it just takes some time to warm up, but its getting there.' Strenuously explaining everything in detail about her instalment of the new British boiler.

In a way, when Gran left him alone, he felt as though every movement was being listened to and observed, as though he was supposed to be free to do what he wanted, but knowing he couldn't, she would never understand him really. He was alone with his inexpressible feelings and experiences. The entire purpose built retirement settlement of bungalows was listening and pretending not to. Whether Gran was asleep or in the room with him he felt alone. Never quite understanding what people meant by the expression that when they were being watched it meant they weren't alone, or vice versa.

That night he slept in the single bed that his grandfather had died in a while ago. The thought of it didn't make him feel uncomfortable at all, to the contrary it gave him a sweet feeling of company, a vague, perhaps imaginary memory of trust in another.

Trust was difficult to experience. Once, many years ago, he found that he took it's lack and it's presence for granted. What made him take notice was a terrible sense of loss, as if the only person that would have left him to do as he pleased, encouraging with true acceptance and direction, had gone. What he felt was that something had happened to his grandfather; he hadn't realized that, throughout his life, a relationship had been building that was quite unlike any other that he had. He found himself crying stupidly for the first time in over a year, for reasons unknown. Two months later he was in bed, watching television, when his mother had come in; he couldn't remember the words that she used, but she told him that Grandad was dead.

Without emotion he watched the rest of the film, and he made love to his girlfriend for the last time. It was as though he was bestowed with a mature awareness of how badly things were going, that no other teenager would have noticed.

He, Gran, and his mother sailed out onto the Solent and threw Grandad's ashes into the silence. They hadn't bought any flowers, instead they had broken some from their garden as though it would be more appropriate, more personal. The sea rocked the boat, but not enough to keep them seated. The current took the flowers which they had flung into the sea on top of the ashes and they lost sight of them quickly. He took the wheel when they decided to return. All he had to do was keep the front of the boat pointed at one landmark and it was easy. The wind caught him in the face and dried any tears, but he needn't have hid them anyway because steering meant he didn't have to look at anyone. It felt like getting on the sea were Grandad's last wishes and he felt proud as he sailed his mother and Gran back to shore.

From then on he only ever cried when he thought of Grandad, always with love and the feeling of wanting to make him proud and at unexpected times, like when he watched documentaries of the war.

That night he dreamt he was a child again at his grandparents house, number nineteen Dilly Lane. He was up an apple tree that seemed huge; he never actually saw himself in his dreams, only seeing things from his usual perspective. In his arms were a bow and arrow that his grandfather had shown him how to make out of bamboo and string, the arrow was severely disproportionate and outsized the bow.

'Grandad!' he shouted, as Grandad walked underneath. Grandad looked up and he shot him directly, bulls-eye between the eyes.

He woke the next morning to the sounds of his grandma pottering around the house. Strangely she wasn't talking to herself, as though it needed his presence, as though it needed him to be there.

Often when he woke up after a dream he would harbour the conclusive feeling throughout the day, and sometimes longer, but that morning was different, he didn't feel any guilt, as if he had never been punished for shooting Grandad in the face.

Christmas day was to consist of a trip to a nursing home. Gran wanted to see an old friend of hers there. Gran didn't have many friends, none that she ever saw regularly or spoke to for that matter, most of them had passed away years before. She said she hadn't spoken to Margaret in a long time, at least a year, because of a dispute they had, since when Margaret had moved into the home.

They drove down the small coastline roads, it was a beautiful sunny Christmas morning and the air was sharp to the nostrils. He reminisced to her about things he could vaguely remember in the landscape and she filled him in on what he had done there as a child and why such memories would be vague and fragmented. Often she was astonished when she would ask him if he remembered certain things and she would receive a negative, embarrassed, reply. But he was inquisitive and content to find out what he had done, the games he had played. The gaps were being filled in, and he could generate vivid pictures in his imagination. Nothing outside their small world of memories was discussed.

Driving along the shingle drive towards the home, parking clear of the designated ambulance area outside the main entrance, he noticed how few cars were there. Gran explained how Richard Branson's gran was staying there, coincidentally, almost as if she could see his sad feelings towards nursing homes in general and she was trying to make this one seem nice and caring. He helped her out of the car and fetched her walking stick from the back seat and kept her stable as they walked over the shingle. Once inside a nurse greeted them and inquired who they were there for, then led them into the lift and out towards the main living/assembly room. On the way Gran whispered discreetly to him that they wouldn't stay for lunch. He didn't quite understand why, had they planned to do something else?

'I'll bring her, you can wait in there,' said the care assistant. So they stood, uncomfortably, in a room with six silent residents, staring like them at the countless Christmas decorations that had undoubtably spent more years in the home than they had. The decorations hardly able to provide the uplifting atmosphere that they were intended for, they needed as much care as the "prisoners" did, and were probably brought there for much the same reasons; he couldn't help but feel the reason was to be forgotten.

It felt like ages before Margaret arrived, when she came through the door he felt stupid for being so narrow minded. It was as much effort for her to move her Zimmer-frame as it was to move her foot, and needed the full cooperation of the care assistant and Gran to sit her down. He felt so out of place and clumsily unhelpful, feeling that he ought to be helping, but he was ignorant of such matters. He could see that Margaret was overjoyed to see them, but he was closer to tears than she was, there was a purpose for him to be there. She had known him when he was little, the last time they had seen each other was twelve years ago, a fact emphasized by Gran repeating it continuously.

All his memories of her had completely disappeared, now he wished he could remember, that would give them something to talk about other than how amazing it was that they hadn't seen each other for so long, or wish each other a Merry Christmas. A few minutes later Margaret asked him what his name was again.

He told her again, trying not to look too disturbed. Again she asked how long it was since they met again, slightly excited, but as though she wanted to be reassured? Gran saw what he was about to say and intervened. It wasn't just that they didn't know what to say, Margaret's memory wasn't lasting every long, and age had taken its toll.

All the other residents were watching by this time. Gran and he were their visitors as well, no one had come to visit them, Christmas had turned into what every other day was, just another one, except they were supposed to be cheerful. The happiness wasn't being provided and he was starting to feel guilty by focusing all his attention on Margaret and not on any of the others.

An employee came and handed each of the residents various presents provided by the establishment, wishing them a Merry Christmas. He was glad that the silence had been broken, but his gladness ended when he realized that the presents were meant to compensate for all the gifts they should have received from their relatives or loved ones. Each of them got different things. A little bottle of cheap cologne that would never be worn because they never went out, or a bar of soap that would never be used because they couldn't wash themselves. Washing was done in a very mechanical way, as efficiently as possible by the underpaid staff.

Margaret was shaking far too much to open her present. Before any of them reached the possibility of becoming upset by the unbearableness, Gran snatched it out of her hands and, pretending to be enthusiastic and excited like a little girl, opened the parcel to reveal nail varnish and lipstick.

'Would you like us to put them on you,' said Gran knowledgeably. Handing him the nail varnish, 'you can look pretty for lunch with the boys?'

He hadn't a clue how to apply nail varnish, but was far too self consciously polite to argue, besides, he really wanted to do something for Margaret, to cheer her up, however absurd it might be. Margaret nodded at least thirty times. He held her delicate hands softly to keep them still, and

Gran put some lipstick on her. Margaret's eyes, without blinking, stared straight through her. Meanwhile he did the best he could with her nails, the more varnish he put on the worse he felt, he didn't understand what he was doing.

The whole situation seemed uncanny, especially considering that he was now treating his gran as if she wasn't going to be in one of these places quite soon herself, ever, the thought hadn't crossed his mind since they first arrived. Looking at Gran he could see she was fully aware of her fate, she knew what it was like, unlike him she could identify with the residents, that was why she was acting so professionally. She knew how every bit of attention, every drop, was appreciated. One needed to have experienced a void of care, support and company to truly appreciate it. Wondering if the patients had lost so much, but gained something too, even if it was a tiny truth, a perspective that adolescence tried so hard to destroy, ever escaping, denying wholeheartedly.

Pre lunch sherry was brought round, he was offered a glass, but as he watched the others barely able to take a sip he waited for Margaret to drink hers. Margaret looked at her glass despairingly, she knew she couldn't do it by herself, he knew. A few minutes later Gran kindly put it to Margaret's lips that had newly applied bright pink lipstick on. Margaret was immobile so Gran took the initiative and poured it into her mouth. They watched as it just sat in the back of her mouth, her lips making abstract uncontrolled movements as though to help. Margaret made clicking sounds which penetrated the silence everyone had fallen into. Gran stroked Margaret's neck, like a child gets their throat stroked by their mother to help the medicine go down. It took a while, but Margaret managed eventually, and her eyes lit up. He could see the sadness and pity in Gran's face for the first time, he knew she had been courageous but it was wearing off, he wondered if it was time to leave. Then he realized that everything was tremendously difficult and that was why Gran didn't want to stay for lunch. But how would it be possible to leave Margaret courteously, even if she wouldn't remember, even though they both felt they had made her Christmas, was it enough? He could see Gran was thinking the same, he wasn't alone; he was free.

Aware of the solitude of the other residents, together they helped Margaret back to her room where lunch was waiting under metal lids. Margaret's room was bare and exactly the same as the other rooms they had passed on their way down the corridor. It didn't matter for the room who lived in it, it didn't care, the room would always be the same, as if it too was waiting, waiting for the time when Margaret no longer needed a place to stay. Waiting like she was, to be empty.

Margaret asked them what they were having for Christmas

dinner, Gran unveiled the plate and explained what was on it. Stating how envious she was of Margaret's roast, comparing their souffle and peas to her wonderful cuisine that now filled the room with the same smell that all hospital and school meals smelt like. Gran delicately cut the dinner up into tiny indistinguishable pieces and painstakingly fed it to Margaret, who ushered him to sit. He asked who the picture was of on the shelf.

'Oh, isn't he handsome,' said Gran, speaking for Margaret who was only too happy for her to, 'that's Margaret's first son, he passed away in the war.'

It was a black and white picture of a young man with well groomed, parted, short back and sides, the way his grandfather had taught him to wear his hair when he was young. Margaret's son wore a uniform and peered out with a charming smile, it reminded him of his grandfather and made him think of what suffering his grandfather must have gone though during the war. He felt that he owed Grandad, perhaps even all those who fought, to try and contemplate their suffering, even if he knew he would fail; but there was something which made failure acceptable, it would demean a soldiers courage and suffering if it was possible to contemplate, the more alien it was to him the more courageous it made them.

Gran stood up when she felt that Margaret could swallow

no more.

'God bless,' said Gran. Those words that she always said to him at the end of their telephone conversation that always gave him a feeling of gallant sorrow, in the same way that the space shuttle launch commentator would with the words "God speed". But the words "God bless" now possessed a far greater significance than before, now he'd seen the application that was meant for them.

Not knowing really how to depart he gave Margaret a kiss on the cheek.

'Oh, aren't you lucky,' said Gran. The journey back was silent.

Margaret died four days later.

Chapter 2

On his way back to London, back home, he felt as though he had to compensate for making Cherry spend Christmas alone. The thought gave him that feeling one gets when a friend is annoyed but nothing can be done about it. Never before had he been able to call somewhere home, life had always been boarding school, moving from one place to the next. Always making friends with the other pupils he never saw again once he'd left. It seemed that he only ever made friends with them because he had to, there wasn't anyone else, only a finite amount of people, and no escape. Or perhaps they had only made friends with him for the very same reason. Did all of them still maintain a friendship and forget about him? In the same way that you put something away and not only forget where you put it, but forget about it entirely. It was amusing though that all his treasured memories incorporated "friends" from boarding school.

Since school he had been living in London for three years where he attended college, he knew most of the other pupils there, but never seemed to do what they did. He never socialised with them out of college hours, never went to any of their house parties, he was never invited, shit, he hardly even knew any of their names. It didn't seem to matter, he was content with Cherry, all he wanted to do was curl up with her and forget everything else, to fall asleep but have the feeling of a soft presence permeate unconsciousness.

He rang the door bell to their semi in Peckham, not because he didn't have keys, but he enjoyed that kind of arrival, that kind of welcome. The door didn't pull back to reveal an expectant smiling face. Cherry opened the door in her usual indoor kit of enormously baggy trousers and woollen jumper, never ceasing to look elegant. Instead of a smile came a brisk "hello". She turned her back as she walked into the living room that was only lit by the television. He followed her inside and watched in silence as she climbed onto the couch and pulled a duvet over herself, only interested in the obscure program that they had become accustomed to watching together.

He put the flowers he brought her into a vase and put them in her line of sight, directly in front of the television. As soon as he had retreated into the kitchen, she got up, sighing strenuously, loud enough for him to hear, and moved the flowers just enough so that the telly was visible. Then sat back down in exactly the same position, reinforcing the insignificance of his gesture. He knew there wasn't any point in asking how her Christmas had been, he knew she had worked through Christmas eve as a care assistant in a nursing home. Never aware that their Christmas's were profoundly similar, it would only have served to reinforce the fact that he wasn't there for her.

The house was in the kind of chaotic mess that Cherry made and that would make him annoyed. He was constantly picking things up after her, and if she did ever clean anything it would take her forever, he would manage to hoover three rooms and the stair case in the time it took her to wipe the kitchen table and side boards. But this time he picked things up without making a fuss. He made as much noise as he could with the washing up, by throwing things into their rightful place instead of placing them carefully, to attract as much attention as possible.

Because her mess was the only presence of hers he could obtain, it made him feel as though she wasn't completely remote. And so he indulged himself fully in her material presence.

After about half an hour of unnecessary noise making, he realized it wasn't going to work, so he found things to do that would need him to walk in front of the television. If she wasn't going to hear him then at least she might see him while he pretended not to care. The plan usually worked, but always involved some kind of hostility, and it depended on her speaking first, then he could apologize for whatever she told him to. It also meant that he could, in some way, present a weakness in him that she might feel sorry for, thus distracting attention from what had happened to something she might see as more important. But this time he just couldn't quite persuade her, there was something more important that she wasn't mentioning.

He apologized.

The next morning breakfast was silent, Cherry moved into the living room after she had finished and he followed her obediently, as if awaiting instructions.

'I feel lonely,' said Cherry. 'Nobody tells me that I am beautiful anymore.'

'Why do you have such a need for people to compliment you, why do other people count so much, why do they matter?' he asked, echoing many discussions they had before. He knew why, but didn't think it would be healthy to state the fact, again.

'You are always watching me with other men, I can't do anything, I can't flirt, everyone's careful when you are around. You are always so serious, they make me laugh and give me compliments. I just don't feel pretty anymore, I don't feel wanted. I want to meet people and right now I don't feel I can do that.'

'What are you saying?' He knew very well, he could see what she wanted and that she didn't want to say it; she wanted to be like she was before, she wanted to go out with other men, but he wasn't going to say it for her, he wasn't going to give her that. Right then he didn't want to give her anything at all. So he just waited. He stood and gazed down at her.

'I want to see other men,' she said in a quiet voice, trying to sound accompanying.

There were so may things going though his head, so many words and thoughts, so many emotions. He was thinking quickly. Each time he thought of something to say it led to another. Each sentence transformed into another before he could voice it. She waited for him to say something, he knew she was waiting and it made him think even more. Everything he thought of was so potent, it meant so much and it was so scary, he was too afraid. He felt as though everything he might say would sound stupid, he couldn't find the right words for his feelings, for the exhaustion his whole body was feeling, for the confusion that he was feeling. He couldn't even repeat that he just didn't understand.

However long it took him he was going to think of something mature to say that would resolve everything, but he was taking so long and the longer he took the more mature he had to be, the harder it became. He thought she knew what he was feeling and he had to say something that she didn't know, he was searching. There were questions, replies, answers and demands, all seemed to string together, and the whole possible conversation, including outcome, was repeating itself.

'What are you thinking?' asked Cherry.

'What?'

'I can't read your mind?' This time in a more demanding voice, but with a tinge of cynical hopelessness.

After a while he felt like she should understand, he was paralysed, he wanted her to pressure him, he couldn't say anything. He couldn't remember if he had said anything or not. There was a stupidity in starting back at the beginning of the conversation that he had experienced, for some reason he thought he had experienced. For some reason he took it for granted that she had experienced it as well. He took it.

He was as far as the "making-up" stage and just wanted to lay himself in her arms and fall asleep, but didn't dare move in fear of making things worse. Instead of trying to articulate his feelings and explain them to her, he forgot about them and tried to figure out how to patch things up? He hoped that if he waited long enough she would ask him how he was feeling in a way that meant he only had to answer yes or no, if she asked enough questions in that way they might eventually come to a conclusion. It meant he wouldn't have to think about it, it meant he wasn't saying it, she was and he wouldn't be responsible and to blame if it eventually went wrong. He didn't want to say anything because of the risk involved, he wasn't thinking about the particular moment he was thinking about the consequence.

Cherry asked a question, but he didn't hear what she was saying, only that she was giving him something, perhaps opportunity, at least that's what he thought at the time.

'No!' came his answer in a scolding voice. He didn't care if the question was correct or not. He just wanted to say no in a way that put her down, a "no" that would sound, to her, like she knew nothing, she hadn't a clue. Careless if she was right or not, he always felt less mature than her, but he was going to appear as though he was more mature. He didn't care if she never thought that he was immature. He was going to make it seem like he was the better party. Lying didn't matter.

Shit, she could always speak her mind, he knew she was

better at it than he was. He always felt less than her, even when he first met her he thought she was way out of his league, although he never admitted it at the time. What he was feeling was that she was better than him in every way, but that would be the last thing he was going to say, that would be like handing it to her on a plate, it would be like committing Kamikaze, perhaps worse. For him she was prettier, more intelligent, older, more mature and, more importantly, she could go out with anyone that she wanted; she could ask anyone and she wouldn't be refused, and that was what she was suggesting right then. No, he was going to do everything in his power that was going to make him feel better than her.

'Do you still want to be with me?' he asked finally in a voice that sounded like she would have to do a lot if she did. He managed to feel like he had the upper hand by making the sentence seem unfinished, like he was going to add "then" at the end.

'Yes,' said Cherry, in a voice that sounded feeble to him.

'Well I can't be together with you if you are seeing other men!' he said this trying to sound as seriously genuine as he could, demandingly, the last half of the sentence he spoke in the crudest voice he could muster. Without voicing it, he wanted to make her feel like she was a bitch.

'Is that it then, is it over?' And she began to cry. He wasn't going to show any feeling, any emotion. He watched her for a while from above, as she sank into the sofa and curled herself up and hid her face with her hands. After a while he sat down next to her and stroked her hair, comforting her, but all the while, maintaining a distance and a definitive status.

He had done it, he had made her shrink in comparison, after all he had split up with her not the other way around, he was in control, he had made the decision. He had made it seem as though something had been taken away from her and not from him, almost a part of her, even if it meant losing everything that he wanted. He knew she could manage without him, that was what angered him, because he felt he couldn't, but he pretended he could have a life on his own without her.

For the rest of the day he thought there was a hope of her backing down. If he acted independent, self confident and outward-going, maybe his security would draw her. He maintained that what he was doing was justified and virtuous, that staying in on new year's eve and celebrating at home, if not funny, would be artistically amusing. It was difficult though, everything he did usually involved her, he didn't have any other friends. There wasn't anything significant he could find to do, but his loss was well concealed, he thought. A day of nothing passed by, a Cherry void.

That afternoon he decided that to show his maturity and insanity he was going to get completely pissed for the new year celebration. So he drove to the supermarket and bought a bottle of tequila, to serve as a warm up, and a bottle of Champagne to be opened at midnight. Driving was something that made him feel superior and mature, every time he got in the car he thought people would look up to him, it was something that Cherry didn't have.

He cooked them dinner and they spoke again. They had to discuss living arrangements, it could have, should have, been extremely emotional, but he spoke calmly and evadingly.

'We are such good friends,' he said, 'we have tried living with other people and it always fucked up, we live so well together, there isn't anyone I would rather live with than you.'

'You are my best friend and I don't want to lose you, I'm afraid that if we live separately it will be the end of our relationship.' Cherry replied.

'I want to live with you, it's so nice to live with you.'

'Yeah, we can still be best friends, we just won't sleep together, or in the same room.'

The relief came after having been thinking the worst all day and it wasn't necessary to mention anything. The thought of Cherry going was so terrifying, that he might be on his own. Alone, he would have the responsibility for the house rent and the cat, but he didn't want to mention any of his insecurities, in case it would give away his weakness. There were so many practical things to think about, he felt it would be impossible to manage. Besides he knew that there wasn't going to be another man in Cherry's life for at least a while. By leaving it he could sound like he could deal with the eventuality. Most of all he dreaded the thought of beginning on his own, starting with nothing and having to work so hard again, seeing it as being worse than living with an exgirlfriend. This way he would have to deal with it all later, and what he wanted most was not to think about it.

The tequila was opened and there were just the two of them together, giggling and talking shit. Whenever they knew they could stop laughing for long enough to concentrate they would pour another tequila, spilling half of it and fall into hysterics because of their inability. To him it was all sentimental, some of their best times together had been the same, it was a kind of ritual and he hoped it was making her feel the same. They fell over laughing when they realized they were watching others celebrating in Trafalgar Square on television.

They kissed and for him it felt different, he felt the kind of fear you feel when kissing someone you just met, a sweet kind of clumsiness, hoping that the other person is enjoying it, numb to how the kiss actually feels. Somehow there was an element of trying to win something over. Now she wasn't his anymore, but it was more than that, it was something they weren't supposed to be doing, they both felt sadness, fear and guilt all smothered by alcoholic dizziness and laughter. It took a bit longer than usual for them to be undressed, he had to wait for the moment when he was absolutely sure that she wanted it. Every now and then their laughter would interrupt their love making, always preceded by a clumsy action that would make them both physically uncomfortable.

Normally he was soft with her, only taking gentle strokes, but somehow he wanted to show her that he could do what other men could, so he tried to make it more passionate and aggressive and they moved around the room as one.

Cherry started to cry, held him hard and stopped him from moving. It was difficult for him to join her in sorrow, mostly he felt an anger just above his heart. They lay there for a while not moving, just forcing themselves together, he tried to force a tear for her, but all he could muster were shiny eyes, which he didn't hesitate to show her. It wasn't about sex, it was about being together, totally. He knew she was absolutely focused on him and he could think about the day's events without sadness or fear, like they were all hypothetical.

The count down on the television interrupted, he wiped the tears from her face and reached for the bottle of Champagne, still looking into her eyes. On the stroke of zero he popped it open without leaving her. He poured some into her mouth. Then he took a sip, but didn't swallow, and withdrew from her.

'No!' shouted Cherry in the voice she always used when he was going to leave her prematurely.

He smiled reassuringly and went down on her. From his lips he blew just a little Champagne into her sex.

Chapter *3*

A dusty sadness loomed over the next few months. There were so many new rules that were unspoken, but neither he nor Cherry knew how to orchestrate them. Every time he looked at Cherry he could see that she had so much to say. Why wasn't she saying anything? Was it because she didn't want to give him the wrong idea? Suddenly she couldn't say "I love you" anymore. Everything she said sounded different, it all sounded careful. Was it that she didn't want to hurt him?

Sometimes he would forget that they had split up and would hug her from behind when she was doing the dishes, or when she was brushing her teeth. For a while she let him, but as time passed she would remind him that wasn't what friends did. It never really sank in. Why was it that before she loved his touch and his hands and now she would remove them? So he used different ways of touching her, different reasons. Instead of caressing her bottom like he used to, he would slap it and pretend that it was a joke, laughing dismissively when she became annoyed. When she would walk up the stairs in front of him he used to put his hands between her legs and used her walking to stroke her sex. Sometimes he would put his face in her bottom, allowing his nose to push in between, feeling her cheeks moving over his, but he couldn't anymore, so instead he would just push up from behind her.

Every little bit of affection seemed much greater, at the same time as every neglect became far worse. The list of phobias soon included sleeping alone. They would sleep in the same bed sometimes, it only happened if Cherry had spent the day with him and enjoyed it. He learned to ask if they could spend the night together at the right moment, but more and more frequently he was refused. All his efforts to do more things for her didn't work. He would even wake up at six in the morning to pick her up or drive her to work to get a "thank you" and a kiss from her. The kiss would linger on for a little longer than she thought it ought to, she seemed afraid to fall for him, she would say she was just unaware at those moments and would apologize for what she had done.

Sometimes they would still make love, it happened quite unexpectedly, he was never the one to initiate it. Sometimes it happened in the middle of the night when they were in bed together, but usually she just grabbed him when she wanted. He could never refuse, sometimes he would, but he never meant it; he was just trying to show that he didn't need her for sex in the same way she did, but she meant it, and besides it never took her very long to seduce him. It was always passionate and strong, with pulling and scratching, as if there wasn't much time. There wasn't really any foreplay, clothes were never off before he was inside her. On occasions she would have her panties off and he would have to force her legs open to get inside her, she would struggle with all her strength until the last minute and then devour him, giggling all the time. It felt so strange, it was so beautiful to kiss her with everything he had, but as soon as it was over he knew he couldn't touch her. It would make him happy for the next few days. As often as he could, he would completely immerse his face in her sex and then walk around college and smell her with every breath that he took for the day, wondering if others could smell it too. It excited him to think that others could, but might be too embarrassed to comment. He loved it when she bit him on the neck, when she did he wouldn't let go, pulling her and asking her to bite harder, he loved the strength of sensation, it would also leave a mark which he would never disguise. Knowing she didn't want it he would do the same whenever he could; giving her a love bite when she was unaware, preoccupied with their love making, scratching her back when she was coming and unable to speak or move, or perhaps oblivious to the sensation. He was proud of the marks their love making left on her, it meant other people would notice, and it meant she wouldn't forget, he prayed she wouldn't notice and cover her neck and back. When she did notice she was always angry, he apologized each time trying to sound as sincere as possible.

He didn't feel that much had changed, except for them sleeping together. He still saw a lot of her and living together meant they had a lot things they were both responsible for. She was going out with new friends that she had made, and it upset him to know that there were things she wanted to do that didn't involve him. It upset him too that she was making more friends than him, she was less inhibited and more outward going. To him it seemed that everyone liked her more than him. When she introduced her friends to him, he was critical of them and it made it impossible to get along with them, she hoped so much that he might share her interest in them, but he couldn't. He couldn't approve of them. For Cherry it meant that there was something in her he was disapproving of, it was true, how could he like her interest in others. But he would never dare to say that he was jealous, which would be a sign of weakness. She wasn't jealous of him and the last thing he wanted was to be worse than her. So he always found a rational reason for his dislike, a justification for a feeling that didn't really exist.

Whenever somebody asked where his girlfriend was he would explain that they weren't together anymore, emphasizing the fact that he was the one that had left her, and not, remember, the other way round. He would say it jokingly as if it didn't mean so much, in a way that would cover up the emphasis. One night she didn't come home, his fear kept him up almost all night, he was conjuring elaborate events that might have forced her to stay at a friend's house. Perhaps she had gone to a party and missed the train back, perhaps she didn't have enough money to pay for a taxi?

He wondered what he was going to say to her, how was he not going to sound jealous, maybe he would just be angry with her for not calling and telling him she wouldn't be coming home. He could say he was just angry that she let him worry about her, but he never really wanted the call in the first place. That would mean the loss of the hope that she might eventually come back, that it wasn't just a long party. The night was spent restlessly trying to fall asleep and not feeling jealous and awaiting her return. The feeling though, which really prevented any calm in his stomach and made him need to use the toilet, the feeling which tortured the most was realisation that the relationship was over. It had taken something like that to prove it, it was indisputable evidence. A sadness which might have served as justification for anger in terms of fear, but as he wanted to appear confident, like her, would have been contradictory. If only she wouldn't come home, ever. He wouldn't have to worry about confronting her, but that would feel as though she never existed. He could never rely on his wish that everything would be the same as before, that was all he wanted, and if she hadn't existed then there might not be anything at all for him.

The next morning he checked her room, just in case she had come back when he was asleep, but she hadn't. The bed was the same as when he had stood and looked at it before he went to bed, wondering if he should sleep in it or not. It was so nice to sleep and not think about all the shit, he turned around and went back to bed, this time he couldn't sleep because he was wondering if he should go out or not before she came back. Then she might think he didn't care what she did, he might look independent, but he was going to see her eventually anyway and try as he might he couldn't think of anything to go out for. In fact he didn't want to go out, he didn't want to do anything.

The unlocking of the front door woke him up like an alarm clock, set because you want to wake up at a certain time, but you never want to get up when it eventually rings, the latch was set to ring. Cherry came straight up to his room.

'Hey,' said Cherry, meagerly.

'Hey,' he replied, looking away. Somehow without his willingness the pace had been set, he wasn't going to show that he cared.

'You want to know what happened?' she asked, making his heart race.

He wanted to know, not what happened, but that she hadn't slept with anyone and even if she did, that they hadn't had intercourse. But he was disgusted that she was so willing, so eager to tell. 'No,' as formally as possible, looking away. 'No, not really,' sighing. 'You can tell me if you really want?' he said, shrugging his shoulders and trying as best he could to sound disinterested.

'We didn't have sex.' She looked at him for a while as he tried to occupy himself.

He couldn't believe she knew exactly what he wanted to know and he tried not to look surprised. 'No,' he said almost trying to sound sympathetic in an "oh, too bad" kind of way, not wanting to say much at all.

'No, he wasn't going to use a condom, but I told him I wasn't going to sleep with him unless he did. You know, he tried to tell me how much he hated them, he tried to persuade me that they are shit?'

'I don't see the problem, so many guys think they are shit, like you can't feel anything at all, I don't mind them. So.'

'So he went to find one and when he was putting it on he just threw it away, but I knew he was just trying to cover up that when he was putting it on his dick shrank and he couldn't.'

'Yeah,' like he knew about such things, but it never happened to him. Actually he was shocked women noticed things like that, they could see what was really going on, that excuses were being made. She might have noticed all his excuses as well. Even though she had been with another man he felt strangely happy, he could compare himself with the other man. This guy might have had her over night, but he was still better, he was the winner, he had been more intimate with her than anyone. For a minute he forgot that he could never have it again.

They didn't really speak about it again after that. He thought about it all the time, she didn't stay out at night for a while, so if they didn't converse about being separate then he might find comfort, a kind of uninterrupted daydream. But Cherry was hiding herself from him, she would get upset if he came into the bathroom when she was taking a shower or getting dressed. She even wore underwear in bed, something she hadn't done since they had been together. He never saw her nakedness, somehow it made her more appealing. Her underwear became increasingly irresistible. Her belly, which was beautiful, brown and protruded over her low trousers just enough to fill both hands, became inviting. More than ever her strong, spicy smell would arouse him. He had never met a woman whose smell was so animal and intoxicating, other women would wash and hide their smell, but Cherry didn't, her perfume was so similar to her sweat it only made it stronger, and she wouldn't wash for days. He remembered that when he first met her he found her smell so curious, it was like wondering if her perfume tasted like it smelt and couldn't help licking her armpits. But now there was a difference, he couldn't have it, he couldn't have her. He didn't want others to smell her, he was positive that if they did they too would become aroused, so he just became annoyed and told her that she stank and should take a shower. Hoping that it might lessen the chances of someone being attracted to her.

He couldn't help it even though he knew that his actions might be preventing her from being as attractive. He wasn't achieving what he really wanted. He was slowly driving her away, each time he criticized something about her, although he disguised it with justification, an excuse of some sort, like she looked too provocative, he was in a way insulting her. She started to ask his opinion less and less, he knew he was driving her away, but he couldn't give her what she wanted. She missed attention and compliments, he knew that was why other men appealed to her and why she hated being single, why she was searching, but he just couldn't give her anything. When things went his way in life she would be happy for him and celebrate and hug him, but he hated her happiness, no, he wanted to make her jealous. He wanted it to sound like things were going better for him than her.

He thought she wouldn't make love to him again, when she did he was overjoyed, there was still something from him she wanted, there was even a slight feeling like he had won a prize. It didn't last very long.

'Listen, I'm sorry,' said Cherry, getting out of his bed afterwards, picking up her clothes and holding them in a bundle in front of her breasts, covering as much of her body as she could.

'Wasn't it nice?' he asked.

'It's just so desperate, like we're too afraid of losing something, I didn't do it because I wanted it, it was like I needed something. I hate that, it was just like trying to be extreme and it was so full of fear.' It didn't make sense, she wasn't making sense. 'All those things you said, and it didn't last long, we were running to find something that wasn't there. It isn't there!' And with that she left.

He stayed in bed for a while, it had all happened so fast. She was right he had said something to her, it made it hard for him to remember what had happened. He had told her he loved her. He remembered he couldn't help himself, it was such an overwhelming sensation and he had wanted it to last forever. That was the first time he had been able to show his weakness since they had split up, somehow he had felt secure. He never wanted to tell her how much he was still in love with her and had managed not to until then, it had just slipped out. It had all gone wrong, what he had hoped to achieve by saying that was to make her feel the same, but it had scared her.

'We shouldn't make love anymore,' said Cherry later that day.

'Why do you?' he asked after a short pause.

'Because you are so good,' that was exactly what he wanted to hear, for a moment it made him forget her rejection of him, 'but I don't want to give you the wrong idea, to get your hopes up. It's just sex and I need it sometimes, it's just physical. I don't love you in that way anymore, I love you as a friend, but just because I have sex with you doesn't mean I'm in love with you.'

It made him feel so small, he could only get what he was given. She could have what she wanted. How could she separate sex and love in that way? It made no sense to him. He had never been able to do that, for him it was a sign of love, if he had sex with someone he was showing his love for them. She had demonstrated her power over him, but she was sorry she was abusing him. It wasn't necessarily her fault, he had asked for it, he should have been able to say no, but he couldn't. He was going to take what he could, even if it misguided him.

'It doesn't give me false hope, I'm not stupid you know,' hoping that what he said might make her think that he, at least, was alright, and leave it open so they might fuck again. When was she going to stop thinking that he couldn't take care of himself? He thought that there might come a time when it didn't feel desperate. Maybe next time he could be slightly more aware of himself and not say such things, it might feel nice for her then, not scary.

Normally she would tell him when she was going out in order to invite him, but after a while she stopped altogether and he could only go out with her if he invited himself. He would catch her at the last minute, all dressed up, and ask her where she was going, knowing full well that she couldn't say that he wasn't allowed to come. If she did refuse him, it would be a sign that she was going to meet someone and she wasn't yet at the stage where she was confident or unsympathetic enough to admit that.

One day he asked her if she was going out, she said yes, but told him outright that he couldn't go with her. He asked her why not. It took a long time for her to start explaining. He could see that she didn't want to, she didn't want to hurt him, but neither did she want to be dishonest.

'Well,' she answered eventually, after obviously wondering what to say, 'I have met someone really nice and I really like him and he treats me so well, he respects me, not like you. There are things which he doesn't like about me, but he doesn't criticize me, he respects me. He lets me do things my way.'

'What's this fucking respect thing, what do you know about respect?' That was how he felt genuinely, he really didn't understand. He also knew that she had never left when they had an argument and it always lasted long. It might make her stay. She left and he could see that she was angry. She had never been angry enough to do that to him, she always took his aggression sympathetically and thought it wasn't directed at her. He tried the same thing over the next few days, sometimes even when she wasn't going out, she just became less and less tolerant. When he realized what was happening he tried to be nice about her new lover, by asking her questions about him, and it made her happy, but he was still trying desperately to find a fault which would prevent her from falling in love. All she wanted for him was to approve of something that she did.

'He is a really nice guy, you know. I think you would like him,' said Cherry.

'Yeah,' he knew he could say more, but he didn't want to.

'You know, I can never show him my home, it's like he can't see what's really me, my stuff and how I live, or cook for him. I'm never with him in my environment, it just isn't comfortable.'

He thought that was good, at least some sort of alienation, but his feeling was too immature to voice. 'Well bring him over, I will stay somewhere else for the night,' avoiding the word painful and trying to sound as mature and independent as possible.

So she called Alex to come around for dinner.

That night all he worried about was what Alex looked like, was he better looking than himself, stronger, older?

It wasn't hard to find a place for the night, he knew someone that went away every weekend to see their boyfriend, but he hated the idea of having to leave his flat for Cherry. It was obvious Cherry was going to have sex in the room next to his. The intimacy and privacy felt so incredible, like he was giving himself away. He told Cherry that he was going to be out for the evening, but he was so curious. So he went home, pretending to do something so as not to give the wrong impression. Cherry opened the door and smiled at him, in an embarrassing manner. She was going to find this difficult, but she couldn't say anything because she had wanted them to meet. Besides, he didn't want to make it easy for her.

'This is Alex,' she said, making a kind of laughing sound and shying away. Alex walked in and ducked under the door. Alex was huge, making him feel weak and redundant; now he felt like that was what all women wanted, nothing like an average small weak man, like himself. His determination to make any kind of relationship for Cherry as hard as possible, and to make Alex feel as unwanted as possible, only grew. His ability to deal with the situation as well as possible was the only way that he was going to compare with Alex, and that meant not being, or at least showing jealousy.

Cherry introduced them. He asked Alex all the things that he thought were polite and expected. All the while feeling the stranger himself. He had never felt so foreign around Cherry before. He persisted with niceties and thought that cooking them dinner was about as far as he could go. None of it was for Alex though, everything was done to impress Cherry. He made a curry, it was what he was best at, it just had to be good. He felt that if it was really good then Alex might even have to compliment him on his food, a compliment would mean he had won.

Cherry and Alex didn't speak much, apart form saying that his food was great. He couldn't eat, he didn't want to, but if he didn't it would be letting down appearances. It was so revolting. Normally he would have another fork full before he had even swallowed, but now he had to concentrate fully just to be able to swallow. In the same way that he had forced the food down, he forced himself to stay and made himself sick like an amateur bulimic; he forced himself to say that it was nice to meet Alex, but he had to go. Everyone looked around trying hard to find something to focus on, struggling hard to forget why he was actually leaving.

Even though they knew why he was leaving was because he was jealous, he still made sure that no one saw him take the duvet out of the house, as if it would make a difference.

It was freezing outside, but he had to breath so he wound down the window. Each breath was staggered in the same way a sigh is broken in sadness, or in the way a young child cried. At the lights he had to push the seat back in order to take the pressure off his squashed, contorted stomach, to relieve the heartburn.

When he arrived, he had to shit so badly it made it almost impossible to open the door, there wasn't any time to find a light switch or to walk to a street light in order to find the right key. The first thing he did when he got inside was rush straight to the toilet, leaving the door open in his clumsy desperation. He sat there for a while with his eyes closed, allowing his breathing to be loud enough for him to hear, knowing no one else could, unable to move. On opening his eyes he found himself in front of a window that rose from the floor to the ceiling.

The city was spread out in front of him in miniature, the tiny lights twinkling beautifully, from a safe vantage point he could see everything that he wasn't a part of. It seemed empty, deserted, but every light was representative of at least an activity, he knew they were doing something, but didn't know what. He hated the curiosity, if only it would go away he might not feel so lonely, for a second that was what loneliness meant, but the lights were hypnotic and wouldn't let him go.

Then he noticed his own reflection in the window. He was projected out over the entire city. It might have been a tolerable situation, was he not in the kind of situation that nobody really wants to be seen in, with his trousers down. The thought was bearable until he reached for the door and found he was unable to close it.

He walked around the house to try and find something to occupy himself with. It was impossible, there wasn't anything to do, it was almost empty, practically a showroom. He couldn't shrug off the feeling that he was being shown a flat by an agent, a flat which had recently been renovated and it's history of occupancy eliminated.

There was a beer in the fridge, as he drank it and sat in the bright fluorescent lit kitchen he remembered what he would always say about drinking on one's own. The flat was so cold the beer didn't give him any sensation of warmth, he would have to drink much more than that. He fumbled around with the boiler for a while, but didn't have the patience to work out how to switch it on.

He ran a bath which took ages to fill. The sound echoed all over the house. How beautiful it was to be submerged under the bath water. It gave him the feeling that shutting his eyes couldn't because he could still hear, sounds were so difficult to eradicate. It was complete rejection of everything outside, at most only allowing a dampened down version of the truth, perhaps taking a bath would allow him to persuade himself that things weren't as they were.

The phone would ring, never for him.

Unable to wait any longer he jumped straight in. It was swimming pool temperature, but he was going to sit it out anyway. It only aggravated his tenseness, if he didn't move he wouldn't be able to feel how cold the water was, but he had to move to keep warm. He didn't get out because that would be like admitting how shit the situation was. Submerging himself wasn't of any comfort either, he hated the silence and it's elimination of company. And he realized that the only noise there was came from himself.

He was wet and colder than before. At least if he was with someone they might laugh and joke sarcastically about the situation, but he depended on someone else to be able to do that. He put on all his clothes and got into bed, curling up underneath the duvet and breathing heavily to try and warm up.

Chapter *4*

'Thank you for letting Alex stay over, it means a lot to me, that was really generous of you,' said Cherry.

'Well,' he said, shrugging his shoulders as though he was being asked a question.

'Alex was really impressed with the way you were, how nice you were to him,' she could see that he was only trying to be above it all.

If she had said the same before it might have been enough for him, it might have been worth it, but now he felt that if she didn't want him. If she wanted someone else, then he wasn't going to provide any opportunity.

'Well I'm not fucking doing that again!'

Cherry didn't understand and he wasn't going to explain how terrible his night had been. An explanation seemed like an excuse to him. The excuses weren't working anyway, at least not the way he wanted them to. They weren't bringing her back to him. Perhaps his jealousy might, maybe his real feelings would show her how much he loved her, but he hated his jealousy, he hated everything he did. He couldn't find anything to do, nothing that made him happy. He thought that if he was jealous or angry he would have to show it and through it, and only through it, there would be some kind of escape. So he explained to Cherry how she had made him feel abused. He spoke calmly, he felt it was at least a start, unconfident of where it might lead, ignorant of however useless it might be.

'Cherry, you can always go to his house, but I can't just go so he can come and take my place.' He didn't want to say that he just couldn't bare to hear her fucking someone else, but he had to, if there was to be any substance to the argument. Sick of being empty, he hoped his anger and jealousy might give him something to be. So often he had found himself envying other people because they had a friend or girlfriend and he felt left out. They had something to do, something that gave them a name, something that gave them a status. 'I only left because I didn't want to hear you having sex with him.' It wasn't the guy he dreaded to hear, *her* sounds of pleasure made him feel sick.

'He wouldn't make love to me in our house, he respected

you too much. I didn't really understand because you weren't even there, but he envied the way you dealt with things.'

He knew that he wouldn't have done the same for Alex, it was something he could play on, he could use it against them.

He didn't know why, but that night she invited him out to a bar with a few of her college friends that he had met once or twice before. Perhaps she was offering some compensation for the previous night or, even better, she had seen something in him that she hadn't before, some sort of merit, a maturity or an independence. He didn't feel like going, he wasn't the kind of person that went out regularly. Small talking with strangers was arduous, lingering silence uncomfortable, relevance was all that needed saying. But it was a chance to set an example, so he agreed. She told him that Sofia was going. Sofia had kissed him before, although that was a long time ago, maybe he could make it happen again. It might even make Cherry jealous, even if she had never presented herself as a jealous person before, a characteristic he never understood.

In the club he met Mario and Sofia and they all found themselves on a couch together in the brightest corner. He bought them all drinks as some kind of gesture, he had a straight whisky before his beer, making sure they all saw him drinking it in one. He had seen men drinking like that somewhere and imagined it would do the same for him. They were all squashed on the couch together, touching and he wished he was sitting next to Sofia, so he might have an excuse to touch her.

He and Mario watched Cherry and Sofia dance together closely, laughing. He wasn't confident enough to be able to dance with anyone, even if it was just for fun and it wouldn't matter how good he was, dancing was always a contest, and there was always an element of self-conscious ability. When they were tired they fell back down on the couch on top of him and Mario, giggling and oblivious to what anyone else might have thought of two girls dancing together so closely. He tried to hold on to Sofia and squeeze her in next to him, the visibility of his actions prevented him; he wasn't clear enough and she moved back to the other side of the couch with Cherry.

Mario commented on the wonder of meeting people that were generous with contact. He hadn't noticed.

All these people knew about him was what Cherry had told them and it was making him feel uncomfortable. What had she told them? Mario had told him that he wasn't as arrogant as Cherry had made him seem. What else had she told everyone? Had she forgotten everything he had done for her, if only the practical things? In what way was he arrogant? It was true that anything anyone mentioned he had done or at least new something about, he didn't really know any other way, the thought shut him up for a while.

Suddenly Cherry and Sofia started kissing, it was more than a friendly kiss that he was used to her giving other girls. It was so spontaneous of Cherry, she seemed so accomplished. How could she be so spontaneous and carefree? He could see it impressed Mario no-end. It made him feel pathetic, he couldn't take any initiative. Mario complimented Cherry's savage uncontrollability, words which had come to make his stomach crease, he had felt sick quite frequently recently.

Cherry, Mario and Sofia enjoyed the games they were playing, they didn't mind what other people thought. If that was how they were going to have fun then it didn't matter, but it made him cringe. He was speaking less and sipping more. Mario got up to go to the toilet. The girls said how funny it would be to find out how big Mario's dick was, urging and pushing. To him it was a stupid idea, but he wasn't going to refuse the girls, he needed to go to the toilet anyway, and he wanted to be part of the action. At the urinals he couldn't really work out why he was there, how had he been persuaded to take part in such a stupid plot?

He stood at the urinals and struggled to say something funny, feeling slightly exposed himself and trying to avoid any mishap. He finished before Mario and left without saying anything. On his return the girls just laughed, they didn't seem very interested, perhaps the joke was on him. Could it be that they just wanted to get rid of him for a minute or two? He laughed anyway, pretending to understand. Whichever way it was going to turn out he was going to be a part of it, following as if he knew where it was leading. When the club closed, they decided they would find somewhere else to go.

They crossed the road and entered a dark basement with modern furnishings which didn't quite suggest a time or an era. It was practically empty and there were mostly men whose dress or style didn't give them any vocational indication.

When the girls were dancing, Mario leaned over and without looking at him, said that he wasn't able to pee if there was someone next to him that he fancied. Mario moved close. He knew exactly what was going to happen, the situation was the same as when he wanted to kiss a girl. It was a safe way of making yourself available, it left little evidence of what you wanted when it didn't work out. He kissed Mario, not really confident of what to expect. Their kiss didn't start off softly and then develop, it seemed hurried. Exactly what it felt like was elusive. It was nice not to have to make any seductive effort. Mario didn't expect him to be strong or tall, but he couldn't help feeling like he was being treated like a female. It made him feel courageous, but he didn't know what the reward was.

The kiss was going to go unnoticed, so he held on long enough to be sure that the girls would see, worrying about what he looked like embracing a man. He had rivalled the girls in his efforts but he was unequal because he was only inadvertently experiencing these things, all he wanted to experience was equality in itself. He couldn't work out if one depended on the other. He could remember what he had willed, but if it had turned out differently, as it had, was all conclusively the same? Did Cherry feel the same as he did in his spontaneity, did she enjoy the experience, or was it just the spontaneity itself, if so was it enough, did spontaneity justify itself?

No mention of a kiss ever came. Hardly surprising when he thought about his reservations about others spontaneity, everyone was taking revenge on him for his own dismissals. Mario asked him if he was gay, he told him that he had been quite homophobic some time ago and never understood why other people told him that meant he was afraid of his own sexuality. He continued to say that now, for him, there were simply beautiful women and beautiful men and no one could say they were strictly gay or straight.

Mario followed him upstairs to the bedroom. Normally he would make an effort to disguise his intentions, even if he was usually happy with the outcome, he was still embarrassed. If he concealed his intentions then he could always maintain that the outcome, whatever it turned out to be, was what he had planned all along. He didn't ever really know what he wanted exactly. Frequently he would spend time not noticing it's passing, spending time contemplating its fate, what was the most economic way, what were the consequences, which one was worse. He was unable to think about one thing at once, everything was always interconnected with everything else. If there was the possibility of asking someone else's advice he would never let it pass. There was nobody to ask this time, of course there was, but he didn't have the courage. What would he ask? He didn't know what he wanted, it was just happening, it was happening to him, he had made himself the victim. There wasn't any time. So far he had been out of control, but there wasn't anyone to blame. Was he just going to withdraw even more? Did withdrawal mean continuing with things as they had been going so far, or did it mean eliminating himself from the situation entirely?

He got into bed and Mario had followed.

'You can sleep here, but I don't want to have sex,' he said to Mario. That was the first time he had ever said such to anyone, although he had been on the receiving end occasionally.

Mario didn't say anything, he just lay down. It reminded him of what he had done in similar situations as Mario; he would pretend to have no expectations. But Mario was different really, he thought, for Mario sex was far more trivial, going to bed meant having sex. He couldn't imagine there were such innocent things in Mario's life.

'You like Sofia don't you?' asked Mario.

'Yes,' he replied. Not really wanting to say more. He felt like he had become completely uninvolved in the situation by eliminating any possibility of development. A conversation would only drag himself into it once again in a way that would leave little room for escape even if it was meant to create a distance. Everything he had said that night was to give himself an appearance of being in control. Now he felt stupid, as if his insecurity was visible to everyone, like he no longer had secrets, like his orders weren't being listened to, like they sounded foolish or were in another language. He was the newcomer, he had never done something like this before, how could someone in his position be in charge? How patronizing he must have sounded.

'You're stupid,' said Mario, acting as if he had been rejected for a legitimate reason, 'if I were you I would be next door with her.'

Mario's status was growing and it was alarming, not only

was Mario telling him what to do, but Mario was also commenting and being critical of his confidence. Mario was telling him that he was incapable of overcoming his fear of rejection, bringing his worthlessness to the fore. Had Mario been aware of his passiveness all along, using it to advantage? Vulnerability became an issue.

Only then did he realize where Mario had referred to. He could hear the girls in bed together next door, giggling. Part of their amusement must have involved him and what they thought he was doing with Mario. He would be entertained if it was someone he knew in his own position. Somehow his position seemed far more earnest than theirs, even though they were all novices, he felt like he had far more to lose than they had. Maybe it was because their reason for being in their situation was more legitimate than his? What was his reward going to be? He felt like he had invested far too much for what he wanted.

Mario didn't seem to mind that he was thinking about Sofia and Cherry. He took the opportunity to turn around and try to fall asleep, it might be the only opportunity he was going to get. There wasn't any chance of getting out, and he had little enthusiasm of going into it even more than he was already.

'When you're sleeping, I'll rape you,' said Mario quietly and politely. As if it was an ordinary thing to say.

He wasn't worried perhaps as much as he should have been. What could he do about it? It made him kind of happy that he meant as much to Mario. At least someone was noticing him, thinking of him, wanted something from him or saw something in him that he could give to them, something that no one else had.

After a while, when he was nearly asleep, Mario wrapped his legs around his and started to stroke his back. There was a possibility that Mario could turn him on or make him hard at least. He concentrated so as not to give Mario an excuse to carry on. With every stroke of his back he twitched nervously, like someone was breathing on his back and it was tickling. Worst was the hairy legs around his own, it was like putting two of the soft sides of Velcro together and expecting them to stick.

Although lying there and not denying anything was passive, it was a different kind of state than he had been in before, earlier it had been more emotional, he hoped this kind was more defensive. Mario's legs around his brought up memories from a long time ago, he blamed himself for those experiences. Yet he was putting himself in the same kind of situation, not really knowing how it would affect him later. He wished that his earlier experiences didn't affect him, not that he would forget them, that was impossible, but that they wouldn't resurface at times like these. He had enough on his mind as it was. He was feeling very young again and quite vulnerable, but it wasn't Mario's fault, how was Mario to know. He felt, for only a second, that he should tell Mario, but the compulsion vanished as quickly as it had arisen. He never told anyone about those memories, not even his mother.

How was he to manage sleep? How was he going to feel the next day? He knew that he didn't want to see Mario the next day, if he did it would be conformation of what had happened. He hoped that he would never see Mario again and, hence, forget everything had happened. He imagined an entire scenario of what the next morning would be like, what he was going to say and what he was going to be asked by Cherry.

He awoke later to see Mario walking out the door and the girls peering in. To hide his confusion he smiled and the girls got into bed with him, one on each side. Had they been planning it for a while? How long had he been asleep? What had Mario been doing while he was asleep? Why had he been unable to go to them? How come they were able to come to him, was their courage multiplied because there were two of them?

Cherry left after a while, he didn't really understand why, but it was in key with the rest of the nights events. He couldn't ask her to stay. He didn't really know what to do with Sofia, he didn't feel sexy at all, but he couldn't help feeling that he was supposed to. With Cherry sex was easy in a comfortable kind of way, they knew what each other liked. He didn't want to be alone and it was nice that Sofia was there with him, but he knew she felt as awkward as he did.

Woken by his own kissing, he found himself tightly clasping Sofia. He knew it wasn't an excuse, but in his dazed stupor he made love to Sofia until he was fully awake. Sofia seemed to appreciate strokes that were quite different to what he was capable of. It wasn't about giving at all, Sofia just wanted sex.

For days he mentioned nothing of it. Everything he did was permeated with his bewildered memory of his night with Sofia, Mario, Cherry and his disbelief. When he did see Cherry again and it came up in conversation, his memory of what had occurred was so vague. She asked him how it had been. The harder he thought about it the more things would slip his mind, the more he would wonder what other people would think. He didn't know what to make of it. He thought he had learnt quite well to express his feelings, but it was as if things had just happened to someone else, like it was all a rumour. Like someone had told him their experiences, but had forgotten to include any emotion, like they had given him a report and now he was supposed to tell Cherry. He didn't reply incorrectly, he didn't reply at all, at least not adequately.

It was different for Cherry, she was happy with what had happened, she had got what she wanted, she had been present, she had made it happen. That wasn't the reason she was talking about it, she wasn't exited for him, it wasn't about something they had shared, it was about something she had done on her own. And he knew nothing he could do would persuade her otherwise. The night had meant enough for her to tell Alex, who Cherry said was jealous. So nothing like that was going to happen again.

How had something that he had let himself get into, something he hadn't asked for, at least not directly, that had meant to make him and Cherry closer, done exactly the contrary?

The next few days he felt empty and intolerant, the days were as uneventful as his feelings. He wanted to feel like he had done before, even that was better than he felt now. How he had felt before that night had happened had become the norm for him, a quality to control, anything else was unexpected. To achieve his wish meant undertaking as mundane things as possible, it also meant avoiding Sofia and Mario. He didn't want to be distant to enable himself to comprehend, however bad it meant the consequence was going to be.

He woke up a few days later, after a night of drinking, to the sound of the telephone ringing. The enthusiasm to speak to his mother had increased; he knew she was going to call that morning. They spoke for a while and he pretended that everything was fine, he repeated the word, almost without saying anything else, managing to keep her on the phone without saying anything in particular. It was strange. She was the only person who might listen and understand, but the last person he wanted to know, whose judgment really mattered, the only person who might even take his side even if he admitted being a traitor. At least that was what he felt every time he gave himself the space to think about confessing, not that he was looking for an answer at all, far from it, he refused any answer outright. When she did finally catch on that something was bothering him, all his definite thoughts seemed trivial. In the end he just felt lonely. The only reason he could think of was that he missed Cherry, but as soon as he admitted it he automatically denied it. It triggered something inside him which he couldn't hold back, like being listened to was actually drawing it out of him. He didn't want to cry, but he couldn't help it. With deep gasping childish sighs he told her how he missed being with Cherry and how jealous he was of her. It took ages for it to come out, he had to keep repeating things so that she would understand. Perhaps it wouldn't matter if she didn't, there wasn't anything she could do about it. Everything was pointless. It must have been the desperation which she picked up on which made her ask if he wanted to go away. Going away was something he hadn't thought of, it was a good idea. He said yes in two staggered parts.

He took some of his attention off the phone for a second and noticed Felix, who had crashed at his place for the night. Felix was staring at him from under a blanket. Shit, he noticed how he had been more than crying, he had been sobbing and it made him feel naked enough. But he had, in his eagerness to get to the phone, forgotten to put on any clothes. He was crouched in the corner, naked, crying, pathetic. There was silence and, as he wondered what Felix must be thinking, he hastily said goodbye.

Chapter 5

He woke in a deep sweat. He hadn't remembered it being so hot, it was terrible. The fan was on full, but for it to make a difference he had to lie directly underneath it, naked. The fan was hypnotizing, it made a beautiful sound. If he followed it with his eyes as quickly as he could, he might just catch one of the blades for an instant. Gazing preoccupied him for at least an hour or so.

Being in a different country meant he should get up and go out, so as not to waste any time. But he felt moving would be wasting time, appreciation would be difficult. He had arrived so quickly. The truth was all that made him feel like he had travelled was his exhaustion, apart from that he could still be back in England for all he cared. He was still thinking the same things, they were still bothering him in the same way. No, that wasn't quite true, they were annoying him slightly more because they were so far away and he couldn't work out how they could stretch so far.

The more he considered what he had run away from the less he felt like going out, but the guiltier he became as a consequence. Going out also meant instant recognition of arrival by everyone, the thought of standing out made him feel uncomfortable. All he wanted to do was to slip past unnoticed, perhaps that way he could also forget where he had come from. He hated the period of arrival which he always felt, it was always the same, he wondered if other people had the same experience. Maybe he could just spend a few days out of people's sight in the apartment, then, when he did finally meet people he could say he had been there for a while. Alternatively he could lie, but it wouldn't be the same it would still take him ages to do anything, he would still dress inappropriately, feel disorientated, he would still be ripped off by the locals.

He picked up a book that the last tenant had left, something about a golden bomb, German expressionism without any punctuation. At the rate he was reading it would have been simpler to stare at the fan, at least then it wouldn't matter if he lost his place or not.

There was some fruit in a bowl on the dresser, even his hunger gave in to his reluctance to go out, so he ate the fruit incredibly slowly.

The next day was his birthday. It didn't seem important, no one else knew, but he was glad to be twenty. He remembered being seventeen, when he had been there before and made friends with an American guy who was twenty-one called Thomas. Thomas was the first man that he thought he might be in love with. Never once while he was around Thomas did he have recognizable sexual feelings, only after a year or so after they had parted did the question of sexuality come up. Thomas had made a big impression on him, he envied how easily women were attracted to Thomas, it was as if Thomas was actually making them fall in love. There were different women every night, never missing anything, Thomas was everywhere at the same time. He thought he would be the same at Thomas' age. Perhaps it was all going to start, but wasn't life gradual at all? Thomas was still his only comparison with what life should be like at that age, at least the only one he bothered to make and valued at all. Somehow he felt like he wasn't supposed to value anything, like Thomas hadn't, couldn't have. If Thomas had then there wouldn't have been a possibility of progression from one experience to the other so easily. Nothing traumatised Thomas in the slightest. Even the misery Thomas so adamantly experienced could hardly be believed, it had to be pretend, a sham, supposing it was another way of attracting?

He thought that age would eliminate misery somehow, it meant being able to comprehend things with more ease, it meant putting things in perspective. But all it had done so far was to give him more perspectives and, as far as he could see, that meant more possibilities for misery and that couldn't be a good thing. Life meant new experiences, it didn't matter how hard he tried to focus his view, there were always more perspectives. He might forget some every now and then, but they would always return after a while; with them they would always bring a new suffering that he wasn't quite able to comprehend: confusion.

The first thing he did was go out and rent a motorbike, it was a better idea than looking for the people that he knew who might be there as well. He found a nice little bike after bargaining for ages and drove around, tediously, until it was dark.

Nothing excited him, he didn't want to do anything if there wasn't anyone to share the experiences with. Somehow he depended on there being someone else, all motivation came from sharing. There had to be more than observation.

Again he drove around for a while hoping that he might see someone, at the same time pretending he knew what he was doing. It didn't really matter which direction he was headed in, all the roads led back to the apartment at some point.

Then he heard horning form behind, so he moved to the side, but it was strange because he made a point of driving faster than anyone else, nothing had overtaken him for ages. When he turned to look, it was Fiona's face smiling back at his. At least someone was happy that he was there. He had made Fiona's acquaintance there a few years ago, since when she had spent a year in London and they had got along quite well. She didn't stop to say hello, she drove along aside him and they shouted at each other into the wind and the sound of the engines. She screamed happy birthday, which was a bit of a shock because he had forgotten himself. He asked her where she was headed, she told him that she was off to a bar to celebrate her girlfriend's birthday who was her passenger. He had never met anyone with the same birthday as his before. Fiona introduced him to her passenger, but he didn't quite grasp her name. Not wanting to sound impolite he made a face like he finally understood. He shouted happy birthday and that he would be along later.

It couldn't be his birthday, it was hers, but that was okay because he didn't want anything from anyone, receiving anything would only distract him from her. He still couldn't make out her name over the music and he felt stupid that he hadn't remembered the first time. If she was to have meant anything at all then the least he could do was remember her name. Asking again would draw too much attention.

Somebody told him that she worked at the bar almost every night, it meant Fiona would probably be there as well and that gave him an excuse for him to come along. He didn't want to look desperate or anything, but he didn't have anything else to do, he didn't know anyone else at all. What else was he going to do? It was kind of strange when he realized that he only had female companions. He thought that it might bare some relation to the fact that he was only brought up by his mother, he didn't really know. People were already getting the wrong idea that something was going on between him and Fiona, but nothing was going to happen between them.

The next time he went to the bar she served him a drink and refused payment. He sat down with Fiona. Surely after the length of not seeing each other they would have something to say, even if it wasn't interesting it might fill the time. He hated small talk, but had thought that he had learnt a thing or two about it, it didn't make any difference. So they both pretended that it was so amazing that they had met each other after so long in such a remote place. Fiona wasn't interested in anything he was doing, nothing amazing had happened in either of their lives.

Never before had he wanted to consume alcohol in order to forget, he didn't know why he was drinking or why other people were. Did they feel the same? They couldn't all have come there to escape, they couldn't all be trying to drown something? But he felt he might have been thinking a little optimistically. They weren't all just travellers in a remote place, there was something ambiguous about everyone laughing on command, but he did the same because he didn't want to stand out. In fact there wasn't anything that he wanted to do, so why not conform? Sitting and observing would have been alright if he could stop judging himself in the same way he did others when they were voyeurs. All the criticism he was making of others he could apply to himself. It made him feel like he couldn't stay still.

The self criticism lasted for days, it might even have been the same day if he hadn't noticed a pattern to the whole thing, a rhythm. It was a similar routine to the one he was in when he left home, except now his urge to touch someone wasn't simply emotional. There wasn't anyone to talk to, but even if he couldn't communicate through words then at least he might be able to remind, confess, order, agree, reply, even compliment or greet with his touch. Although he found it difficult to articulate his feelings, there were still so many thoughts going on in his head. He knew that it was healthier to express oneself, it was an understanding anyone could have told him, a psychotherapeutic cliché, but he just felt that no one cared. He didn't have any real problems that might catch someone's attention, at the same time he didn't have anything to share. In the same way that he wanted to make a jump into maturity without suffering, he wanted to make a jump into a relationship, even if it was only platonic.

He remembered a place where he and Thomas used to spend most of their evenings, where they had watched the sunset and the river down below, played many games with girls who they had both been interested in, finding out who would actually sleep with them in the end, it was always Thomas though. Time hadn't been enough of an issue to become redundant. Somehow everything would be turned into a joke, it didn't matter what had happened to either of them. No matter how horrific the experience they always managed to tell it as if they had read it somewhere. The worse it was the better. The main thing was that they could confess the experience and it wouldn't traumatize either of them.

He parked his bike underneath the block of flats, wiped the tears driving had left him and stumbled towards the lift. There was something about ascending that he loved, whether it was in an aeroplane taking off or going up in a lift. Going up was distinctly different to going down, so much more could be seen from a height and it was far more silent. It was the distance he felt which he treasured, he felt like looking was justification for doing nothing. Staring around a room or down a street was lazy.

The lift stopped abruptly and the centrifugal force pushed his, already upset stomach into an uncomfortable position. He opened the door and stepped onto a landing and into its darkness. The lift didn't go all the way to the top, he would have to climb a couple more flights of stairs and then there were ladders which went through holes in black ceilings.

He lifted the hatch wondering if someone else might be up there. The thought gave him the same kind of feeling he encountered when he had to speak to an audience. But when he didn't find anyone the feeling remained, unexpectedly. Perhaps he had been neutrally excited about sharing something with someone. They wouldn't have had to say anything, the fact that they had found each other would have been enough. They couldn't have been there for significantly different reasons. There were only so many reasons to find yourself up there and they all included some kind of confused remorse.

The sound of night trains could be heard in the distance, the clattering of tracks. The business disappeared, the feeling of needing to be doing something slowly receded.

Even though he had been up there many times before, the thought of being eight floors up without a banister still frightened him. Vertigo was his only company, it was something he could depend on, something he enjoyed, unlike anything else anymore. It made him feel present which eliminated the feeling of escapism; being present was something which only now he realized he hadn't been. There was always something to be, someone to impress, somewhere to go. This was different, it was immediate and he tested its legitimacy by sitting on the edge with his lags hanging over.

As he looked down, he wondered what it would be like to hurl himself off. He wasn't afraid, only difficult things were scary, but this was easy. All ordinary thoughts were suspended for a while, it felt ordinary. The only senses he took any notice of were the physical movements that would be needed to walk over the edge. It wouldn't take anything at all.

Turning his head, to find the platform that was suspending him, he remembered how he had made love to a girl, years ago, on that same roof when Thomas was also there. How much had Thomas seen? If only he could be as unashamed now, it seemed the shame was what was debilitating him now. But how could he be subjecting himself to it, to himself? What was so difficult? It was all the same as stepping off that roof, nothing more, nothing less. Futile.

Everything that he had ever been ashamed of was still with him, he couldn't shake it. Sometimes it seemed like he had, but it always emerged at one point or another, if he didn't remember then someone else would, his gran always had something he was ashamed of up her sleeve. All the shame was congregating in his head as he stared up at the sky. He couldn't help feeling that someone else knew all his secrets, no matter how hard he tried to keep them safe. Somebody had betrayed him, they must have. Someone had divulged everything he would gladly give away, but only so as to be rid of it all. People always told him that confession was a way of healing, but it didn't seem to make him feel any more innocent. Telling wouldn't make him forget, besides, he hadn't told anyone anyway, but they still knew.

No longer did he want to notice people's knowing eyes, they made everything so difficult. He hated that everyone knew more than he did. He didn't want them to know about him, but at the same time he wanted and desired intimacy with them. For intimacy to be real he had to be honest.

'I'm here, you're not, meet you at the bar later, love Fiona, she really likes you,' read the message he found on his door when he got home.

That was right, he had got really drunk the night before and told Fiona that he really liked her friend, in a way which indicated Fiona should tell her, to find out if she felt the same. It was exciting and it made him happy, yet now he really had something to lose. For a while everything he had been thinking about was a result of her.

Fiona told him that her friends name was April and he was determined to remember this time. Fiona also said that April would be quite upset if she found her interest had been given away. He asked Fiona why and she said that April had a boyfriend back home and he was coming in three weeks time. It seemed so far away it didn't really change much. Knowing that April liked him too changed a lot in relation to his feeling of alienation from everyone around him. Materially he didn't have anything they didn't, but he felt like he had so much, even if April hadn't said anything. Each time April looked at him it meant profoundly more then it had before, there was a little secret which they both had, but didn't share.

He watched her move swiftly behind the bar, always smiling. She was so radiant, every man gazed as she moved passed them. Her breasts were so ripe, everything about her just shone.

After the bar closed, he waited for her to clean up and then they went to a cafe. He sat opposite her. He couldn't really say anything and he wasn't hungry at all, but he just had to be doing something. He spent a lot of time trying to preoccupy himself, but he felt so empty. All he really wanted to do was watch, humbly. He wanted to say something, but everything he could think of sounded awful. Her eyes were so sharp every time she looked at him it hurt, he wanted to tell her something along those lines, but it didn't seem good enough.

The event had embarrassed him, it had disclosed his interest in April without having to say anything. Somehow he felt confident that she understood. He started to see compensation in things that he only saw as being negative before, it was April who had unwillingly given him that as a gift. She seemed to be very alert of all her actions, the kind of things she was able to do without actually doing anything at all. That was something he couldn't even dream of being able to do, even if she was making it up, it didn't matter. Before, being interested in April might have been mistaken with the desire to be preoccupied with something, but now he knew it was more then that. If she was only a tool to occupy himself with then he would never have let himself be so exposed, he would have, essentially, kept a distance. A distance he didn't understand why anyone would want, a distance to what? To themselves?

The next night he made sure that Fiona didn't take April home, making as sure as he could that he had the smallest chance of refusal possible. Even though April knew he was interested, she still needed a little persuading and a lot of patience. After all, he couldn't help thinking that was integral. He suggested, in as quiet a voice possible, that they go to his flat first, where they could drink duty-free vodka. It was the best he could think of, he didn't feel like he had anything to offer. She was older and therefore wiser and many men had made her laugh.

Surprisingly she agreed, what he had asked was so obvious and he hated when other men did the same, obvious was synonymous with bad. But he was grateful, so much so it felt appropriate that he should thank her right there and then. She didn't know where he was staying, but she still walked in front of him. She strode so quickly.

For some strange reason, which he felt stupid about later, he felt he had to prove something by drinking more than her, to make himself manly. He soon found out that it was impossible, she drank very much like a man, as if she had an appetite for something, like it was a vital nutrient. He couldn't help mention it and it made her laugh. For the first time in what seemed like a starved period in his life, his inadequacies were becoming amusing, she knew how to steer them in that direction. For some reason he depended on someone else to do that for him. The entire conversation transpired in that direction. They made more fools of themselves than he had with anyone else he had met in a long time, perhaps even more so than with anyone at all.

Some of the things they discussed, they both agreed, were intricately personal and had never been disclosed to anyone else. He had never had such a desire to confess. She had an ability to listen which provoked him to be aware of himself when he was speaking, it was an ability which he realized not many were able to perform. Not that she had learnt to listen, or that she was really doing anything at all, there was just a mutual trust and a kind of neutral sympathetic empathy. He wasn't allowing her to listen, she just was.

She was so beautiful, but she wasn't making any moves towards him, it didn't really matter. The preciousness of the moment was not constituted by the desperate fear of consequential loss, it was precisely that he didn't feel like he had anything to lose. This was more than he had for a long time. She didn't make him feel sexy enough to overwhelm her, something else did. He liked the fact that she didn't give in straight away, he had to push her a little to lay her down on the bed. He could tell that what was making her scared was that the situation meant so much to her; what was happening meant so much.

He lay on top of her for an indefinable period. It was nice to experience the contradiction of knowing and not knowing. He looked into her eyes for a while to let each of them know what was happening, he couldn't have turned away, her sharp eyes would have torn him.

He knew, because he had been told, that he kissed gentler than most men, but on kissing her he jumped back startled. Learning and adjusting to the way someone kissed had become part of meeting. This time he didn't have to adjust in the slightest, but that wasn't what was so scary, he hadn't even had to make any kind of compromise. She did exactly the same as him. He experienced the same kind of excitement as when he would say something, using the same words, at the same time as someone else. Combined with the clumsiness of bending over to pick something up and colliding with someone, who was doing the same. In those kinds of situations he would normally laugh and he couldn't help doing the same with April's kiss.

When he looked her in the eye she couldn't take it for very long, so he gave her the opportunity to think about it and offered her another drink. It was the only thing he could think of to give him that time between the first, the recognition that comes with it, and the second kiss.

She didn't like to press too hard with her lips, nor was she confident with her tongue. Normally he was so aware of how he was being kissed that he would forget himself, but now he was discovering himself. He was becoming aware of how his own kissing felt. It was the same as when he was speaking to her.

The night was mixed relaxedness, the ability to humour themselves and the potence of being overwhelmed. April held him tightly, pressing strongly, especially her chest. She could combine passiveness with vigour. Everything about her exuded an essence of vanilla, her golden skin, her hair, strikingly, her sex was sweet both to taste and smell. Most of all she radiated a warmth. Just being close to her made him feel like he had been sunbathing all day and was experiencing a slight sunburn, painful, but healthy.

In the morning they talked for a while, both of them staring at the ceiling. He took her out to breakfast and enjoyed watching her eat and smoke. Then he drove her home, he wanted to ask her when he could see her again, but he couldn't. It made him shiver and he hoped she didn't notice. He didn't know why it felt suddenly different between them, but he found himself unable to kiss her, so he opted for the cheek instead. He had kissed his gran and made a noise once and she made such a fuss about it, it embarrassed him so much and he felt the same again.

It made him happy when he found out, from Fiona, that his kiss had confused April as to his intentions. It was nice to let Fiona look at him and let her imagine what he had done and how it had felt. His confidence, he thought, came from the fact that he had given so much the night before. If a woman was passive, it would make him feel awkward, but this time he had immersed himself.

Somehow being with April had given his leave meaning and he realized what he was missing before. Not that he had expected to meet someone like April, but he hadn't known what to do before, he had felt so lonely and vulnerable, now if nothing else happened during the day it didn't matter. Doing nothing was enjoyable. He no longer worried about what he might want.

April met him later with the same kind of silence she had emitted the previous night, whenever she had broken it she would laugh to hide something. Her silence when they made love also reminded him of himself and he told her how silent she was. She said that he was so silent that she didn't think that he had enjoyed it, he replied that wasn't the case and that he was silent because he didn't feel the urge of breaking the peace, as simple as that.

They spent a few more nights together. One night she complained about the mosquitoes and he found himself jumping around the room, naked, to catch them. It hadn't really occurred to him that his sex was erect and that it was dancing around chaotically. Her laughter, which eventually alerted him, didn't seem directed at him, she wanted to laugh with him. The distinction was one that he hadn't ever been able to make, although he had heard other people make it. He had tried to do the same, but there was still, at the best of times, a substantial amount of self consciousness.

It didn't take him long to realize that he was in love with her. He told her, he couldn't hold it inside himself. He wanted to say something meaningful and educational, but all he could think of was that he loved her. It just seemed the most appropriate thing to say, nothing else meant very much. Whenever he wanted to say something new and present, it was always superseded by his will to share himself with her. For that reason the trivialities which he did mention just disappeared into thin air, no one taking any notice. When he did finally say it, she just stood there, in front of him, gazing right through him. His heart was racing so fast it seemed like she stood there for ages.

She didn't say anything, it confused him, he didn't understand why she couldn't say the same to him. All his attention was directed to the thought that she *must* feel the same. He trusted, and knew that she did, so why wasn't she consenting? He felt that he was in the position to tell her that she did. He told her that he knew it and asked her why she wouldn't confess. She sighed, she knew she didn't have any means of escape. There was only so long he could wait, but her patience was far greater than his, she could easily out-wait him. He trusted that her silence was an acknowledgement.

Chapter 6

He loved making love to her, it was so beautiful. He loved hearing her squeal and being fought off by her when he tried to see her sex. He loved that she covered his eyes forcefully when he looked at her eyes for more than a second. If she couldn't cover his eyes, then she would cover her own, palm outwards. He loved her long hair everywhere, falling over her face and into his. It would stick to his sweaty face and fall into his open mouth, suffocating and smothering him. Combined with her pressure it would sometimes make him a little claustrophobic, but he enjoyed it, it felt like they were close.

'I hate it,' she said.
'What?'
'I just can't get close enough to you!'

'What do you mean?' he replied not really understanding what she meant. He thought he was being as open as he could in order that they might be close. 'I know we don't really know each other, that we only met recently, but if there is anything you want to know? Anything? I'll tell you, you know that?'

'I know, it's just that I feel separate from you, I want to get under your skin,' gesturing with her hands.

He knew what she meant, although he had never been able to put it so literally. It was a nice expression. It seemed genuinely innocent and he appreciated her will to be close to him. Moreover she had expressed, verbally, exactly what he had always been feeling.

Before he would have to go somewhere or see something in order to receive memories of certain things, he couldn't do it without some kind of external influence. For instance if something was nagging at him, he could interpret what it was that he was ashamed of, or what had traumatized him in some way, such as the roof where he was able to vividly visualize and empathize with memories of him and Thomas. If he wasn't provoked by certain media then he would be able to suppress any memory, he could deceive himself, almost to the extent that he felt that he had only lived half the time he was supposed to have. He had been managing to deceive himself extremely well. When trauma did come up, then he wouldn't want to deal with it anyway.

Perhaps April's shyness stemmed from the fact that she didn't trust him. Although he enjoyed her sweet games of Hide and Seek, he wanted to gain her complete trust at the same time. When he was around her, he didn't need his and Thomas' roof to bring things up, he didn't have to go up there, April was such a reflection of himself that just by looking at her he had to confront himself. Maybe that was why it felt like there was still a distance between them. Perhaps his past had made a barrier, not only between him and April, although she was of the most immediate concern, but between him and everyone and everything. His relationship with Cherry had been terrible recently, he had treated her terribly for completely selfish reasons. He denied his own shame and because of that he couldn't truly trust himself. If he couldn't trust himself, then, why should April, could there be another reason for her not to admit her love for him?

How was he going to learn to trust himself? If he did, then he might really be able to mean what he said and believe what he felt. After all, as far as he understood, if someone trusted themselves, if they were in a position of acceptance, then they could at least convey a fraction of the truth. A truth which no one could honestly deny.

What would he have to do to achieve a state of acceptance?

He wouldn't be able to achieve it immediately and April was leaving soon to see her boyfriend. Perhaps a few days were sufficient to accept just enough? He knew that he wouldn't be able to forget everything, although that was what he wanted to do, that would be artificial. Spontaneity, he might ably accomplish, without worrying about the consequences. He felt that his memories were integral to his thoughts of consequence, so he would have to confront them wholeheartedly. In doing so, he might exorcise in order to eliminate his memories, which possessed the strongest emotional association and attachment, only then would he be spontaneous.

His dishonesty did not stem from his rejection from a woman recently, it needed a lot more than that to persuade himself that he was much more then he actually was. It was far more subtle and intricate than that. He knew because he had been digging up and delving through his attachments before, never quite reaching the end. Each time he had reached the end, it became obvious it was an end in his ability to confront himself, it became apparent that he had to go further and deeper, each time he found that he resented himself even more. It meant he had to retreat into himself and that meant he had to retreat away from anyone he could deceive. After all, if he was able to deceive someone else then he could also lie to himself and was probably doing so, that defeated the object.

He told April about his feelings. It didn't really take much explaining, she acknowledged that she felt quite the same, although she said that there were other things which she wanted to deal with which had a priority for her.

He needed somewhere he didn't have to persuade anyone. It was obvious that he would always be the same until he stopped persuading everyone that he was something other than he really was. He had to find somewhere that would make the transition easier, from persuasion to acceptance, from acceptance to honesty. Somewhere that would make it self evident that *he* would be losing every time he pretended. Where he was, who he was with, his comfortability made it easy, and he couldn't do it by himself amongst everyone else and their corruptions. He would have to be really alone, experience aloneness.

The night he left, April pushed him into some bushes, kissed him and told him that she loved him.

When he returned, he searched for her quickly, but calmly. A certain desperation had been eliminated, it wasn't the outcome he had expected. In fact he had expected to return more of a person, to be more. It turned out that he was slightly more accepting of whom he was. It didn't mean he was less than what he thought, but other.

He found her in the leisure centre. It was like starting afresh and it was scary because he couldn't take anything for granted. They didn't embrace or kiss, he just held her hand.

'How are you?' asked April.

He didn't reply, he had said so much over the last few days, it all seemed futile. He hadn't touched anyone while he was away, he felt so vulnerable. No one had responded to his presence, no one had been sympathetic. He had been on his own. He smiled at her, but it wasn't directed at anyone specific, it wasn't meant to make him look happy, it wasn't exaggerated, it was delicate and breakable. Without actually doing very much, he gestured that she sit down on the bench in the changing room. He knelt down in front of her and cried in her lap.

'You know,' he explained to her the next day, 'just after I left I realized that I was going for you, to prove that I could. I was doing it so that I could be like my exgirlfriend. I thought that she was honest and that was why she was able to give me credit even when we quarrelled and I did things in spite. At first, while I was away, I was simply left to my own devices, and those devices quickly became what I could least tolerate in my life, the memories I most hated. Isn't it strange how when you are left alone to think of anything, you are haunted by what you most want to escape. For me, it is those memories that I am most ashamed of and I became sad that I was ashamed of what I was thinking. After a while those thoughts disappeared and all I wanted to do was leave. I could see the way out, in fact I couldn't take my eyes off it, it was like it was fucking hypnotizing me or something. Part of me hated what I was doing, but it sort of made the whole thing worthwhile, it was a metaphor, it proved my freedom in a way, you know. It taught me something about escapism. I mean I understood the notion of escapism already, but rarely had I encountered it practically in such a way, or so intensely. It was then that I started to feel a change, that I started to be there for myself. Perhaps I was starting to be. No one was keeping me there, no one was imprisoning me. There weren't any rules, I had made them all up myself, as if I was trying to make my life more difficult, but actually I was only making my life easier. You know life is so comfortable when you know what you can or can't do. When you know what you are supposed to do.

'My position and my aloneness, was so alien I didn't know what the consequence of my actions would be, it was so scary that I automatically presumed what the consequence might be. A consequence meant I knew what to say, almost. Like to get where I wanted to be I had to say things that I wouldn't normally, and in a manner that was unusual. It was like I was imagining someone else saying what I was saying and wondering what it sounded like. I don't know why, but I didn't want to sound sorry for myself, I didn't want to sound traumatized in any way. At the same time I wanted to, I wanted help so desperately. I found it so difficult not to compare myself with others. I just couldn't be on my own. It was a terrible feeling, that seemed to be the main problem, there was just no way that I could transcend it, but I had too if I wanted to develop. No one told me what to say, no one asked me a specific question. I could say anything it didn't matter. I couldn't ask anyone's opinion of what I said. The only opinion I had was that of my own. It seemed that my opinion was far more critical than anyone else's could ever be. In order to overcome this I tried to fool the listener, but I couldn't because it didn't matter to them one way or the other. I was caught in my own trap. So I changed, I started saying things which I thought were relevant. I spoke about my mother and my dependency on her opinion, on her approval. I spoke about my father, but I couldn't say anything about being angry or sad and imposing those emotions on what I said. You know, I find it so easy to change the perspective on things. All the way through it was just me interfering with the production of truth. All I wanted to do was blame someone or something else, but I can't really. I just felt so afraid, most of all I felt inadequate, you know, inadequate about everything. Everything I do, I only do it halfheartedly because I worry about what someone else might think.'

It felt fine that April had been listening motionless, he knew that what he wanted to say wasn't really communicable. He knew that his words missed something, in the sense that they wanted to be something other than they were because they were lacking, besides he was mentioning all of it because he wanted to know himself what he had done, like he was articulating it. Someone had told him, it might have been his mother, that he wouldn't really know what he knew until he actually tried to verbalise it. Before he had spoken to April, he thought he knew something, but now it didn't seem that way at all, everyone must have known what he was saying already, it wasn't anything new.

'You know,' he continued, wanting to say something conclusive and answer what he could see April wanted to ask, 'I can't just not be angry or sad or jealous or embarrassed, but at least I might be able to do them properly. Even though I think they are wrong and superficial, wouldn't it be better not to disguise them?'

The vulnerability disappeared as quickly as it had come. He had felt like he should spend time on his own, but then he questioned why. Hadn't he decided to do what he wanted, to be slightly more spontaneous? He could use it, he didn't want it to sleep his decision away.

He found that it was easier to talk to people that he wanted, he was less afraid of making a fool of himself than usual. Most of all, he didn't worry so much about what other people said and did. So often before he had become annoyed and even angry, he never really understood why, or why they were doing what they did. He still didn't, but it left him at an advantage because it debilitated him far less.

It also changed things somewhat with April. She really started to take notice of him, of his body and his presence. It was as if he had told her to be careful with him.

When they awoke, they were both sweating. He loved her sweat, it wasn't really salty it was more sweet. He stroked her wet breasts and told her how much he loved them. She complained that she sweated so much and he tried to persuade her that it was beautiful, that he loved it when they stuck together and they had to peel themselves apart. He compared the amount he sweated with hers, saying that he did much more than she. April wasn't having any of it, there wasn't really any way he could persuade her about anything for that matter. He would tell her that she had the most beautiful eyes and she would just say no and that he did. They started joking about relationships and how they always turned out. They laughed about how nice it was when partners took each other for granted and ended up depending on each other.

Because they were on the subject, he suggested that they

get married and be like the normal nuclear family, with kids and shit. She said that would be nice with him, but he knew she was just kidding. He was too, but he did find himself slightly disappointed when she shrugged it off so quickly and sarcastically. Whatever he tried he couldn't insert any seriousness into the conversation whatsoever. He was sad that they would never talk about things like that, he started to feel like he couldn't take anything she said as definite. Unless it was about him and his body, nothing was really discussed, only joked about.

On the day that she was to leave to the coast he couldn't really say anything. Whatever he said she appreciated, but she wasn't going to respond, he had learnt that by then. He felt like he was giving so much and getting so little. It was all going in one ear and out the other. If he had been in the same position before, he would have been full of resentment, but he couldn't stop himself from giving to April. He just stuck to her like a magnet until he put her on the bus. He wanted to cry to show her how much she meant to him, but he wasn't able to, he couldn't work it out. Wasn't he sad?

'Thank you for letting me cry to you,' he whispered to her before he said goodbye and had to push her on the bus. He watched the bus move out of the station and waved to her as her window passed. He was conscious of his smile, but didn't know if it was meant to be there or not.

Fiona was there too, up until that moment he had had a connection to her because she was April's best friend, but now he just stood there expectantly waiting for something to occur to him to say. Nothing came. He wondered what he was going to do, he was going to be around for another two weeks. He felt a boredom that came with sadness. It seemed contradictory that he could actually feel a void, he could feel that something that he was missing. Everything which moved him he noticed exaggeratedly, because it was not of his own accord. He didn't want to do anything except sit or lay or stand still, but the traffic, hunger and thirst, heat and breeze all prevented him from doing so.

People who he wanted to speak to before didn't interest him in the slightest. His disinterest made him too aware of himself to just sit there silently. He watched how people around him smoked when they didn't have anything to say, perhaps that was how they felt comfortable doing nothing. It reminded him of April. Smoking was what she did when they collapsed after making love. He bought a packet of the same brand that she smoked and took it home with him.

He lay down, it was nice and cool. He wished that it was skin temperature so that he wouldn't have to feel it. So many things prevented him from falling asleep. Everything did, it was a conspiracy. Eventually he managed, after tossing and turning. Often his thoughts kept him awake, but now he missed April's provocation, emotion.

As if it should occur to him in his sleep he thought that when he awoke he should have thought about what to do with the rest of his time there. He had no intention of thinking of it consciously. Because it hadn't, he couldn't help feeling like there was no set date for him to leave. Like he was going to be there indefinitely. Shit, he hadn't learnt anything new, he hadn't changed, he would still be the same when he left. The only thing he had done was lose. He had set himself up for an even greater fall. However hard he tried, he could not persuade himself that what he had done was constructive.

If he wasn't going to do anything else then he was going to smoke. He lit a cigarette without being able to take his full focus off it, for fear of doing something wrong and smoked it with the same awareness of himself, even though there wasn't anyone in the room.

The more he wondered how to pass time quickly, the longer it took. How was it that he had had so many beautiful experiences in his room and they were all fading away, the memories were all becoming less and less vivid? It was a contradiction and he knew it, but as he thought about them the more his memories became like what he wanted them to be. It was strange because what made them so special was that they had taken him by surprise and he was eliminating that surprise. The room wasn't special, it didn't really have any character, the character which it did possess was it's non character. So far away form Margaret's room in the nursing home, it too was waiting, like him. The room and he should have been a good couple, he wanted to disappear and the room wanted to be empty. All he wanted was for the time to pass, somehow that would make him feel like he could get on with it. He couldn't help feeling like that would bring the certainty that he was lacking in his life.

That evening he found himself at the bar again. Everything about it was the same, so the same it was stale, the only thing that he had wanted from it had been taken. It offered a drunken stupor, music, flirtation, impartial company. He sat down and waited for them to encroach on him, but they never came. Then he realized what he was waiting for had been April and she was not coming. It was the difference in himself which alerted him to this fact. He had demonstrated that he was the kind of person that could beg. It had made him incredibly angry that despite all his efforts to make April stay, she still left. There wasn't anything he could do about it. But he was still waiting, that was the feeling which prevailed, but he didn't know for what.

How was it that April could be so intimate with him and so focused on him and know that she was leaving, that she was going to see another man, that she could change her focus of emotion so quickly and decisively? His waiting seemed to be tied into this confusion, like he was waiting for someone to explain it, because it had happened so suddenly. He hadn't really thought about it before, sure he had been sad and everything, but he had wanted to put that feeling off, he didn't want to interfere with what he might otherwise experience. He couldn't help feeling like he was hopeless in his punctuality, that he never knew when it was the right time to be doing something, that there might have been a better time. Perhaps that was what was confusing him, or was it what he had done? Someone said that it was too late anyway. Too late for what?

He wondered if the person who said it was too late knew what he was feeling. If they had fully understood what he was thinking. Had he explained himself so well that they could give him objective advice? Even if he had, could they give him objective advice anyway? And if he hadn't, then had they heard all his thoughts somehow? Anyway, why was it that he needed advice form somebody, what was so different about them? If they were different, would their advice be appropriate?

Fuck it, he thought, putting the other persons words into his own, if he couldn't work out something as simple as what he wanted, then he should forget attempting anything else.

Suddenly, instead of being anxiously bored, he started to feel like he should know more for his age. Like he should have done more and in doing so would have been able to work out what was bothering him.

He couldn't help but compare himself with other people around him that he could see. He would look at one person and decide on what was better about them than him and then proceed to the next, systematically. It was the only rational way. His room had spat him out into this. It had persuaded him that this was better, it had cheated him. At least in his room he had found some refuge, there he couldn't see all these things, they were all invisible, at least to himself. The room's walls had protected him from everyone's knowledge of him, but it had deceived him. Had it also deceived him about April? He couldn't go back there, what was he going to do? It was true that it wasn't better than the bar, it was only less worse. Anything other than being alone, even if it involved the corruption of an innocent person, even if it meant the kind of seduction he was so terrified of, even if it meant lying, even prostitution.

'You know I really like you?' he said softly so that no one else could hear and from behind so that she wasn't looking at his face. Without turning she said the same. She must have noticed him before because she recognised his voice well enough to be confident not to have to set eyes on him. There was a slight chance that she might have noticed his surprise, but he thought he looked confident, enough, for what he didn't know. That was just the way people were and the way he thought he should be as well.

That night he didn't really worry about what she might mean, he assumed that it was the same as what he meant. He hadn't really considered if he could go back to her flat, or how far they would go. Normally he would have worried about it, but he didn't mind if they just slept in the same bed or what. Somehow he just wanted to lay down some sort of protection, even if someone would use it against him.

She wasn't asking anything of him it seemed. It was so different to what it was like with April, he didn't have to prove anything, he didn't have to persuade her that he was worthy of her love. Not that thoughts of April came to him that night. Perhaps he wanted to prove to himself that he didn't need April, that there was no dependency. The thought of being alone just made him feel terrible, but he didn't feel like he was just taking, there was something which he could give.

For a while he felt that he did care what others might think of what he was doing, he knew the exact words they might use when being critical. He also thought that she knew exactly what he had been through, what he might be thinking, so he didn't care to explain or ask what she wanted of him. In fact he didn't ask a single question. He thought that what they both wanted fitted together as needs always should. The only word he could think of when he tried to describe it later was "consentual". To him that didn't mean that it was an adult past-time, but that it was innocent. In fact everything she said to him was so innocent that he found it difficult to respond. It would have been nice to while away the time with nothings, but he just couldn't. He felt that he should be able to, he felt like he had lost something. He expected everything to be complicated and adulterated and he wasn't in the slightest bit prepared. Everything, all the ingredients were there to be intimate with each other, but he couldn't shake the feeling that he got when he watched himself. The more he thought about it the less effort he could give to her.

It was like they had both decided ages ago that they were going to be together that night. He felt that he should think that was nice, but he couldn't accept it. He had a slight feeling that it wasn't a mutual event, that he was in control, not her. Control was something that he had wished for, something which age and adulthood would bring, something which people would admire him for. Now he had it, he hated it. He wondered if the time that they had together would compensate for that small feeling of disgust. He did like her very much, he found her very attractive and honest. She was funny in her own way and she wasn't shy at all. They could both be naked in front of each other without feeling exposed. It felt like there wasn't *enough* fear, that there weren't enough unsaid rules and that they felt like they had been together for a long time. They were at a stage they could ask each other if they wanted to sleep together in a polite way, without the excitement and fear of being rejected because they were used to it already. He didn't understand because he thought he was a relationship person and could never understand when people wished to be single, commenting on his status. He loved the comfort and security of only thinking of one person and there being no doubt that they would sleep together. He loved, more than anything, the fondness and warmth constituting a relationship.

He almost forgot what she said when he started to speak again after listening for a while. He had thought listening was something he was good at, but he couldn't help himself, he had to interrupt her all the time, he couldn't help himself but persuade her there was something more important. Again he had to know the topic better than anyone else and wouldn't admit that he was wrong, that would be like saying sorry. To apologize was such a difficult thing to do, sometimes he would stare and pretend that was enough, even persuading himself that was adequate. Accepting that he might be as innocent as she seemed like a loss of everything he had been through. He couldn't admit that everything he had done since he was her age was just an unfruitful waste of time.

Obviously he hadn't wanted to come across as taking her for granted, but there was more to it than that, somehow he regretted what he had done. He didn't debate whether he had enjoyed it or not, but it was just that there was someone else to consider aside from himself. There was just no way that he could give her the benefit of the doubt that she could take care of herself, that she would only take herself as far as she wanted to go, that she would know what she was letting herself into. Before he had to take care of himself, he had always been the younger party, in fact he had never even contemplated whether he might be hurt if he made himself vulnerable by being intimate. Somehow the burden of responsibility for her feelings made it impossible for him to work out what he wanted, to do, get from her, or give to her. He felt a pressure to make a decision, as though everyone depended on him and was waiting for him to make a decision one way or another, paralysed until he did so. All his attention was directed towards the inevitability, everyone was waiting. Talking to anyone was difficult and maintained a clumsiness that he was unused to. Every second was being wasted, every second smoking, socializing, was futile. Fidget.

The feeling of having done so much, cared so much for someone else in order that they might do the same for him was overwhelming. He realized that it had not been genuine, it had, merely, been persuasion. He couldn't think of anything romantic that they might do together. Somehow he felt obliged to suggest one small past time that they might do together as a token of his appreciation. It was impossible, he found himself following her around instead, with each location he retreated more.

But why? She hadn't asked anything of him, there wasn't even the slightest hint that he should offer anything or that he owed her anything. She didn't expect any more than just being in the vicinity together, that was enough, nothing had to be said, they didn't have to kiss or touch. It wasn't enough for him. Why was it that she demanded so little of him? It was he who made complications, in every sense, although he didn't confuse her lack of demand as a reflection of lack of feeling for him.

Chapter *7 (speak!)*

Later that day Fiona approached him with a fax that she had received from April. He asked her what it said. She shrugged her shoulders implying that she didn't know what it meant. He walked away without saying anything thinking about '*fuck*', and '*shit*', and '*back tomorrow*'.

It didn't make any sense at all; he so wanted to know what had happened to April, but he didn't want to ask. He could imagine she had split up with her boyfriend because of him, but didn't believe she would have said anything. Pictures of them fighting on the beach and both of them sulking came to him vividly, but there was no way that he could suggest them to Fiona to receive any kind of verification.

Both he and April tried to pretend that she hadn't been away. They tried as best they could not to be impatient to see each other and when they did they hoped they could jump into each others arms without hesitation. At least that was what he decided they were thinking. He was becoming fatigued by the inability to say what he really wanted. There seemed little use in trying to hide the truth about what had happened until a later date. Telling April later would only make it more potent, would only make it hurt more. Perhaps telling April that he had slept with someone while she was away would prove to her, with his honesty, that all he really wanted was her.

How was he to know that she was going to take it differently? For so long he had tried to persuade himself that honesty was the greatest treasure in life. It didn't occur to him until she mentioned that she should not - that she had no right to - be jealous, after all she had been away to see someone else even after he had begged her to stay. But he did feel guilty even though, theoretically, he should not. He couldn't help it. The fact that she knew was far more important than his guilt, and he decided that if he could relive the situation he would still have told her.

Some might have taken comfort in the thought that they had no obligation to be faithful. He found little sanctuary in the thought, obligation was exactly what he did want, commitment. What April said only proved that there wasn't any. There was a little comfort, although he found it quite arbitrary, in that she was upset. For some reason he didn't try to persuade April not to be upset, thinking that somehow it might bring them together and bring intimacy more quickly. Like an argument can bring forgiveness and a closer relationship, or a deeper trust in a loved one.

'It's like you are saying 'fuck you' to me and I can say it to you,' whispered April, in a way that showed that she was confused as to her intentions.

'Are you pissed off with me?' he asked, not really understanding what she meant because up until then she had looked so calm.

'I don't know, it's just that you said so much to me before I went away and now this.'

'But, I love you, I don't know what to do. You had gone and left me here. I meant everything that I said and still do, but you aren't showing me any of your feelings, what is it that you want?'

'I don't know.'

'Why is it that everything has to change? It just seems pointless to create this distance after all we have been through. Why don't you tell me what to do?'

'I don't know,' she whispered again as if there was an echo.

'You said that a minute ago.'

April stared at him, she thought that he was becoming angry.

'You know that you can wait here forever until it all seems pointless and I will give up and hug you, you know that I can't resist you. I'm not angry with you because you aren't saying anything,' he said waiting for a reply. April's entire body was stiffening, each movement looked awkward and timid. He could see that she was trying to retreat inside herself, that she was trying to find an inner sanctuary, that she was trying to escape without actually running away. Perhaps she thought that it might become easier. 'What is it that you are scared of? I'm not going to laugh at what you are going to say?'

'You are.'

'Trust me, I'm not.'

'There are just so many thoughts and I don't know which one is the most appropriate, which one is right,' said April, laughing afterwards. 'I just feel so young, but I'm not, I'm not like you.'

'I know what it is like inside your mind, better than you think, not that I can read it or anything, not that I know specifically what you are thinking, but I know what it feels like.'

'It's just so confusing.'

'Why don't you just say the first thing that comes? Isn't that always the right thing?'

April laughed again and he wondered whether she meant

that he wasn't right or if the first thing that came to her head was funny.

'Come on. Is it that you are worried that you might hurt me, that you might say something that I don't want to hear,' and he carried on hesitantly, 'please don't worry? Give me enough credit that I might be able to take it.' He could barely make out April's head shaking from side to side, as if the less vigorously she shook it the less the implication would hurt. 'Come on, just fucking say it.'

'Yeah,' said April in a sarcastic tone, implying that she was not a child.

'You know you remind me of me when I was seventeen or so. I don't mean that I think you are that age, but I remember having difficulty saying what I felt. Shit, up until then I didn't say anything to anyone. I hardly even spoke, you know.'

'You liar,' said April in disbelief. Laughing again and making a face suggesting it wasn't true, how difficult it would have been if it was true.

'I know what you are thinking, and you're right, it meant I didn't meet anyone. I only seemed to have friends because I had to, because I saw them every day in boarding school and I had to get on with them. I don't think that if I wasn't there that I would have been friends with them. I mean, since I have left I haven't been in contact with hardly any of them. The ones that I am still in contact with, that I still see, it's so infrequently. I hardly get on with them at all anyway.'

'But you met me, you talk to me?'

'Well I only really got to know people because I had to, because I was in situations where I couldn't avoid speaking to them. You know how bad I am with people's names, well I only learn people's names when it is absolutely essential. Not thinking that emotions were in the slightest bit important, I hated listening to people talking about their feelings. I thought it was a waste of time, completely. And perhaps I got to know you because you were absolutely essential to me.'

April's comment came in the form of a blush. 'But I can't say anything because you scare me so much, I get so embarrassed when you are around,' she cried. 'So if you think that feelings are so useless then why do you want to know mine then?'

'I don't think that any more. I just felt like that because I didn't know my own, I guess I didn't think I actually had any. Like I was neutral. But it wasn't true. Someone taught me that I did have feelings. We used to have arguments all the time, I would just stare, not really knowing what to say, even if I was sorry I couldn't say it. I didn't know how that might have felt to the other person. Me, just staring at them even if I had done something terrible. I couldn't say sorry because I thought it would sound too trivial. When I tried to think of something to say that would have depth, I would lose myself in my thoughts until I reached a point where I thought that I had said something. I was silent for so long and the longer I took the harder it became to speak. I would be making myself more distant all the time.'

'But you are so honest and say everything,' replied April, not realizing that that wasn't the point.

He made her aware the point was what *she* was thinking, not him, by the face he made at her. 'What is it that you want me to do?' he replied as genuinely as possible. He wanted to sound as though he was truly interested in how she felt and imply that she was stupid. 'Would it be easier if I asked you questions?'

'Yeah, I can tell you whatever you want to know if you ask me.'

'But that is what I have been doing all along and you haven't answered one question at all. Do you want the questions to have 'yes' or 'no' answers? Because I can do that if you want me to, but I think it will only humiliate you more than you are.' He appreciated the position he was in, more than anything else he wanted to help April. That was what he saw as being necessary, not what she might have felt about what had happened since they had been apart, that had all but completely been forgotten. 'Doesn't this seem more important than all the other shit, the maturity, the honesty of being able to speak your emotions? Isn't it true that if we could both just be honest with each other we wouldn't have these kind of complications?'

'I'm just scared, I... I can't, I'm frozen,' said April not really understanding that for him that was better than nothing, it was a start.

'Why didn't you just say that before? Don't think that your fear is part of your feelings, that you might need to let me know that you are scared? How else do you think I might know?'

'Because I hate it. I *do* want to speak, do you think that I like to be like this, it's fucking hell!'

'But the longer you leave it the harder it will become,' were his last words to her before he grasped her and hugged her furiously. It was as if all the frustration that had culminated in him was specifically designed to transform into a desire for her, he couldn't help but think that she might have planned for it to be like that. That it might have been her way of drawing him, or anyone else in the past, closer to her, but things can become so close that they collapse into nothing. Perhaps she could not envisage any other way of coping with her emotions. He could see that the last thing she wanted was to hurt him, he felt the same, and their care, or carefulness, had prevented any possibility of a feud, furthermore a separation. What she might not have realized, though, but he did, was that the very inability, the very fear, would not disappear, it would always lurk somewhere and *he* would remember it. He could see that she might forget, or at least wanted to, but nothing had been cured, only postponed. He noticed that it was like the damage preventing oneself from crying would incur. Feeling that it would be pointless to mention what he was thinking because of the jeopardy that might become of his pressurization.

He clasped her tightly, following her face when he tried to kiss her. What he did know more than anything, more than the consequence of what they had been through, was that her love for him was apparent even if no other feelings were. Her love for him was a redundant question.

Again the next morning they lay naked next to each other. Their legs wrapped around each others in a knot he hoped they would not be able to untie. Again staring at the ceiling that appeared higher and further away than usual, as though he hadn't paid any attention to it while April was away. Ceilings bore no fruits when April was not there to fertilise the flowers.

'It's childish, but I love staring at the roof with you,' interrupted April.

'It's blank isn't it, I guess it doesn't ask any questions of you, like I do. You seem to think that all my questions are aggressive in some way, that I'm attacking you when I ask something of you. The ceiling is protective in the opposite kind of way, maybe that's why you like to look at it? It's protective of you in the same way that a father's or mother's or even caring loved one's gaze is reassuring.'

'You question me like you're criticising me all the time. You think that I have so much wrong with me, do you think I'm defective?'

'No, it's not like that. I wouldn't ask those kind of questions if you weren't important to me, if you didn't have anything to offer. You don't realize, but I have so much confidence in you, I can see that all your fear is superficial, and all that I question in you relates to fear, to expose that superficiality and find what is underneath.'

'But you ask me so many things that you make me feel like there is something wrong with me. Like... Like I'm being interrogated and it makes me feel guilty even if there isn't anything wrong with me.'

'I'm sorry.'

'No one asks me questions like that, not the same as you do.'

'Is it possible that me asking questions like that makes you feel so shy around me?'

'It's just...' the sentence tailored off into silence that lasted for a while. The quiet might have enveloped her and her voice or it might have been produced by her.

'What? What is it?' he asked trying to sound as sympathetic as possible, imagining what she was going to say was going to be incredibly serious. It was something that she did regularly, exaggerating the near future without being able to wait. He knew that he was impatient, but couldn't help it.

'I never know what you are going to ask me next, I never know what you are going to say to me. It makes me feel afraid to be around you.'

'I scare you?'

'Yes.'

'But I just want to know who you are. The things that I ask you all seem important. Even if they are scary for you, the things you are afraid of seem incredibly important. I know they aren't things you would tell anyone, but the fact that you tell me shows how much you trust me already, it shows how important I am to you. It's a little bit of a circle, but it's important to investigate fear because it's scary, do you know what I'm trying to say?'

'I know.'

'Am I not important to you?'

'Yes, you are, don't be stupid. I wouldn't be here if you

weren't, naked with you.'

'Well?' he asked as if she hadn't answered the question; there was more for her to say.

'Well, it's just that you know me too well already. You know that I have secrets I can't tell anyone.'

'Secrets from me?'

'Every girl has secrets,' formalised April reputably, trying to make herself sound as average as possible in fewer words, at the same time trivializing the conversation with a half joke, half truth and a full avoidance which he knew she wasn't aware of.

'I know there are things about me that you don't know but I'm not hiding them from you on purpose, it's just that I haven't been able to tell you because I didn't have the time, I'm not using secrets to hide from you,' He could tell already, he didn't need to ask if it was the same for April, it was not. Her face spelt what he thought was true. 'I, I don't understand why?' knowing that she wasn't going to be able to answer that either because, after all that would be answering much more than this simple question. In fact it wasn't a question, but it might have been if it hadn't demanded so much more.

'You *can't* understand. I'm so fucked up, I can't tell you,' said April as though she was apologising for so much more than not being able to say a few words. Realizing that what she couldn't say had traumatized her entire life. For she had been keeping it secret for so long it had gained the weight and shame of time and buried itself under a pretence. What she wanted to do, he thought, what she wanted to do most, was to pretend that what she was too afraid to say, what she wanted to bury, didn't exist, or at least happened to someone else, distance would justify her manner of dealing with them.

'Why don't you tell me, why don't you try, don't you think it will help, don't you think that is more important than anything else?' He spoke unhurried and clearly, trying as hard as possible to show that it was the same for him, even if it was the only thing he was sure of. 'Don't you want to change?' Was she a heretic? He was so sure that change was possible, everything had taught him it was. Now he couldn't believe that there was someone that actually didn't want to and he didn't understand why.

'You don't understand,' she said again, as though he hadn't heard her the first time, 'you are so innocent, so open and sharing, as if nothing has been able to torture you. You can't know what it is like. You can't. You're so lucky to be able to express yourself, not like me. I'm so deceitful and selfish. I don't want to corrupt you. I couldn't live with that.' Through sharing she would inflict eternal inescapable punishment through a modern psychotherapeutic vampirism, turning him into the emotional vampire she knew he was.

'But you can't do that to me, don't think I am stupid or something. I know what I am allowing myself into. I will only become corrupted if I allow myself,' he tried to say admirably and maturely. He didn't really know how to handle what she said, if it was a compliment, or if it meant that they couldn't be together anymore. He didn't realize that his answer was a reaction to the first possibility, it just came out automatically. He was trying to persuade her that it didn't matter if they were traumatized to different degrees.

He tried to stop her from escaping the conversation, but it was impossible without actually saying that she should sit down and finish what she had started once and for all, without actually ordering her. But how could he ask her to say what she couldn't? There was too much at stake, too much jeopardy, even if it was important to him, wasn't just being around her enough; he realized that it was so far from the simplicity which he had envisaged.

Charitable he wasn't, he was satisfied by being around her and he couldn't work out why. What was it that he was receiving in return, what was it that she was returning? All the time he was thinking, she was dressing and all he was able to do was stare. He should have been able to find an excuse to prevent her from going, something which would make her laugh, something which would make her forget what she was leaving for. He wanted to remind her how nice it was with him in that room and that all she could want was there for her.

After she left, he spent the day alone wondering what had happened, what the difference was, how things had changed since she had walked out, how she might receive him when he next saw her, by chance. He hated himself for not having more initiative, for not being able to deal with the situation more decisively. But how could he have made plans when he didn't fully understand what had happened? They both should feel the same towards each other, the only differences had been spoken. The difference between them, he realized, was that he wanted to change. He didn't like the way he was and thought that there might be a small possibility that he might be different one day. She too had admitted truths about herself which, by the tone of her voice and context, she loathed, but she didn't care to change. No, it seemed that she was, perhaps, too afraid to change, far too afraid.

What was it, though, that would make someone despise themselves so fearfully, in a way that would diminish all hope of bettering themselves? Did they despise themselves so much that, not only would they corrupt themselves, but fear they might also inflict the same on someone else. He was well aware of the shame inside himself, everyone must be ashamed, everyone lived in the fear of God or something, something was always God, but he no longer wanted to suffer the terror. It was precisely the fear of shame which he wanted to rid himself of, which made him want to change. What was it that so traumatized her that made her despise herself so much, that eliminated all potential? He knew that he too was corrupt and deceitful in many ways, certainly more than April knew, so what was the difference between his and her trauma which made him, as she put it, more innocent than her and therefore coercible and corruptible?

What, essentially, was the difference? It could only be that she was older and, because of her seniority, had been traumatised for longer. Trauma, he thought, appeared directly proportionate to time. The more time alive, the more trauma and, moreover, the harder it would be to rid oneself of it. Perhaps that was what she was implying by him not being able to understand, that was why she used the word "couldn't" and not "wouldn't". The theory was almost too good to be true and for a strange reason made him smile for the first time since April had left. Wouldn't it be good to catch trauma early, before permanence?

Instead of repelling him from wanting to be with April it made him want to be with her more, far more in fact. That was what she had given him, he had never understood age in that way. What he always wanted was to be older and more mature. If that meant being more corrupted and less innocent that was what he wanted and, if what April said was true, then he would achieve it far more quickly with her.

Chapter 8

April had tried to put him off, but now she realized that it had done quite the opposite to what she had expected.

'I was thinking today, about what you said to me, about being fucked up and deceitful. Even if it is true, and you would know better than anyone else, then don't you think it was a start, what you were saying I mean? You know, that was already some kind of admission. Most other people wouldn't even acknowledge that much,' he said to her, surrounded by strangers, for all of them to hear. He might have seen hope, but she certainly did not.

Over the next few days he turned April into an idol, something which *he* wasn't, but wanted to be. She epitomized maturity and had the semblance of importance, unlike him. She shrugged it off, saying that what she did might have possessed a significance, but only one which represented a negativity. He agreed, after all she must be right. He asserted himself in the same way he had done before, he didn't know how else to be, but he felt far less in control. As if something was steering him, but he could never put his finger on the map it used to navigate, aware of his ignorance, he didn't try to take control.

Everything possessed a subtlety, intricacy, ambiguity, of which the complexity he could see, but not grasp, a perceptible abstraction. He could see that April was afraid, but couldn't work out if that was a good thing or not, if it was his doing, or if it was out of his hands. It might have been something which he was exposing, that was already in her, or something new that she too had never glimpsed. Novelty might be her phobia. He wished he could expose the foundations, what lay beneath her anxiety, what her, perhaps all, worry, fear, anxieties were built upon, but it was impossible to do so without making April afraid, at which point she would always manage to change the subject. Underneath where the foundations were wasn't there strength, didn't all foundations have to be strong, courageous, valiant? Or was there only deception? He had always thought that the best way to rid one's self of something, fear having a priority, a phobia of any kind, was to immerse oneself in it completely, confront it wholeheartedly. So why avoidance? Why?

Not one second passed when they were together that the intensity of being with her, coupled with the confusion, didn't surface. Part of him wished that it didn't, the other thought that it was integral to their relationship. What was the point of being together if not for intimacy, understanding and development? The thought that she might not want the same made him feel more alone. He didn't know how else to operate, how else to be productive. He knew that the harder he would try, the more afraid April would become. He tried explaining, even persuading, to April that her fear was entirely of her own construction.

He wanted to work things out, but that meant friction and might ultimately end in his dismissal. But simply being with her and enjoying her company left him feeling a certain void. His efforts resulted in many episodes of escapism on April's behalf and he would continually find himself having to start afresh. He was unable to define it, but he was locked in a constant from which the only two ways of escapism were either to decide not to see April or to transcend the void.

That they were close wasn't to be questioned, but he thought that they might be drawn together, inward, he was ready and willing to be exactly that. The problem was that she hardly acknowledged closeness. She was so afraid that she might lose him as a result of what he might discover her to be, so, to prevent this from occurring, she was not going to let him get any closer, any more intimate. They held themselves in a precarious balance between what might be, away from the fear of what might be, made possible by a vaccine which he never thought needed to have been invented, let alone discovered and used, abused.

That people wanted to make plans, that they actually did so and willingly, was something he didn't understand, it was too austerely forbidding for him to achieve. He couldn't remember anything, really, his loss of memory affected his judgment, it was as if nothing was really bad, therefore he couldn't really determine what to eliminate on grounds of inferiority. The truth was that he couldn't see past April, she was the barrier between good and bad. What they sharingly partook was a continuum of dancing and drinking and fucking and kissing and overwhelming. It wasn't that the time passed quickly, or that he wished that it lasted longer, it was that he wished he had noticed it passing him, he wished he had time and strength to bid it goodbye. Everything was saturated with the same extreme emotions, the same desire, nothing differed, no frame of reference emerged. No sleep, no soberness, no distinguishable clarity, and definitely no conclusion. It didn't occur to him that you might need one to have the other.

There might have been an understanding of what he needed to do, what was necessary, but something was always preventing it. It might not have mattered so much if what was preventing understanding was visible. It seemed so abstract and to see it meant that it had to be tangible, at least to a certain extent.

He assumed that they might become distant a few days before April had to leave. He could see that it might be hard for her to suddenly be cut off from him, it had been the same for him on occasion. April did try in many ways, albeit subtly, to free herself, perhaps to end things, by creating small dilemmas through arguments or otherwise. But it never really worked, it might have been his persistence or even his devotion and the lack of will to engage in any serious discussion which, ultimately, put an end to all her desperate measures. He assumed that with anyone else she might have succeeded, but because she did not with him, it made him feel almost special in a remote way.

Again he begged her to stay longer. She said that it wasn't possible, but he just couldn't imagine why, perhaps to empower himself in some way, but he never took the thought any further in that direction. He decided to believe that it wasn't so. He knew it wasn't.

Was he *supposed* to be upset that she was leaving him of her own free will, her own accord?

He drove her to the travel agent to confirm her ticket. As he stood there at a desk holding April's hand, he felt he was confirming more than her flight. He was affirming April's will to be apart from him, her disunion, to make an end, to be alone. Why? If it meant being fucked by the other person whenever they wanted, then rape was better than being alone.

April looked up at him in gratitude for being there with her in the agency, with its smiling stewardess characters. He saw his presence more as following, but wasn't going to argue. She fitted right in. He almost wanted to tell her that she did, that she should become a stewardess. He even thought of disguising his remark with excuses, like she would make lots of money in such a career and it would be easy for her to find a job because of her ability and talent. His immanent wish to confront her restrained him, he didn't want to disguise seductions any longer, neither his isolation, he didn't want anything to be disguised anymore. Everybody knew he wanted to, and they weren't going to let him. No, they were all going to smile and then criticize him when he left, like everyone else did. They were all going to offer him everything, like all bureaucrats do, but not let him touch. He could express his feelings, it had been difficult in the beginning, but he had become used to it and was repeating himself over and over. April stared at him again and again, repeating her silence. She could hear, but it didn't affect her, touch her.

It took hours in the cold, air-conditioned agency. They encountered such bureaucracy and proposed numerous variations of destinations and dates. He saw it as an omen, but April persisted, she wasn't going to give up that easily. He had never seen her so full of compromise. Maybe that was his problem? He hadn't realized that there were times to be compromising, and there were times to be stubborn, each one defined strength.

He looked at himself in the plate glass window, he thought he might look different after all he had been through, he should have changed. It was like he had almost forgotten what he looked like. He did recognize himself eventually, when he was able to block out all the sounds of typing and smiling and questions. He noticed how small he was and how fragile he looked. Then he saw himself grinning, horribly, like everyone else, as though it might make him stronger and less vulnerable. What was it about his face that terrified himself so much? He had got what he wanted, nobody was looking at him and he was contorting everything in the right direction, pretending to do all the right things at the right time, not giving away too much, not saying too little.

How he wanted to work things out, to satisfy his desire or

completely obliterate it, to be put down permanently, made inferior without hope, without complex. How he wanted to lose hope of ever becoming more, to feel it's possibility no longer. Had he made enough effort to finally say that there was nothing else, nothing more? He pleaded to his own image that all his efforts had been in vain, had shown him nothing of an imaginary other. He thought that always pretending to be more than what he was had confined him in a habitual constant, but searching for the truth had become much the same and now he wished it would end. Had his life been as superficial as his searching for the truth had been.

He could stay in the cycle, whichever one it was, all he would have to do was kill off all his awareness of it. It would be a kind of compassion towards himself, in a way. What was more interesting was it fitted in with his idea of being emotionally expressive which he had conceived earlier. All he had to do was find the position in which he could be expressive yet unaware of his position and relentlessness. The comprehension felt regressive, was he submitting, surrendering, or conquering? It seemed to be all of them at once, but not quite any of them determinedly. What else would he be killing, what inhabited transcendence?

Trying to seduce April, to make her stay, to make her love, was the same as trying to seduce his fears, shames and memories. They all came, but only as temptation, to provoke a hope of salvation and never stayed long enough to conquer. There wasn't a statement he could make which maintained any substance, the cures he thought he had found crumbled when the shame resurrected itself.

He wondered if after April had left she would encounter, not remember, memories of her experiences with him. How significant would they be? How would she relate to such memories? If she was happy to remember him would the memories disappear as all his good and happy memories had? He both wanted her to remember him fondly, so as to perpetuate her love for him, and for her memories to be of a traumatic nature so that they would persist throughout her life and have an impact that would be far reaching. What he wanted was for his presence to be solidified in her, permanent. The only permanent things in his life, the only things that he was always sure to remember, were the personally embarrassing situations that he had got himself into. Situations that were so embarrassing, that he always remembered them so that he could, hopefully, avoid them in the future. His want for them never to occur again played a big part in the distortion of those memories, making them seem more like things he would want to forget every time they repeated themselves in his mind.

What could he give April so that she might remember him?

Would being her best lover change her? Even if it would, then would she be aware of the change? Would his love scar for life? Could he balance himself in her memories as something traumatically beautiful?

How could he make himself physically manifest in her? He found himself pulling almost everything out of the shelves and from bags and offering, almost throwing at her, desperately hoping that she might take something. Somehow he saw that he was giving her everything he possibly could, and that if she took everything she would finally be accepting him: his things, himself as a lover, the pain that he made her feel, the truth, his immaturity.

April took something eventually, with a little persuasion, but he felt sad that he had to purchase a plot in her memory. The T-shirt he gave her was like an unmarked headstone in her graveyard of memories. Still, she could always throw it away.

He wanted to make a last desperate attempt to make sure that she would never forget his love. It had to be something momentously romantic, something, almost painful in its reach, where they would almost both experience the same thing together, and that they couldn't experience without each other. It had to be other than what they had experienced before, it had to be other.

'Do you want me inside you?' he asked trying as he might

to be romantic.

She nodded with her eyes not quite fully open.

And they lay there together, bound, spending their last moments together motionless, unmoved by any previous events.

As he put her in the taxi to the airport he felt as she did when confronted with her feelings. There was just so much to say, too much to prove to her, nothing came out, the shock of confusion, real confusion, the kind experienced with loss, built its own little maze.

The taxi moved away into the noise that he wasn't a part of. He watched it and hoped that she was stealing their baby from him. He wished he had made her pregnant with something she could, unlike his T-shirt, never give up, ever.

April was gone, the constant which had manifested itself through the trauma he had been reliving with April was shattered, or so it seemed, but perhaps a new one was gathering itself and would present itself once fully buried under a new awesome manifestation.

It was a kind of resolution, not an end, but a beginning of what he had forgotten. What he wanted was to understand, to know exactly what he was, or what he was in, whether it was April's phenomenon or another. The problem was that he couldn't come to grips with what it was. He was glad and relieved. He had been given something that he really wanted and over indulged himself, and become sick of the taste, it had become disgustingly sweet and overpowering, like anything sweet does when too much of it is had, and it remained in his mouth and on his tongue for ever. Now he had to settle for an unseasoned life, however much he hated it and let it set its own standard, become used to it.

The problem was that it wasn't a specific problem that he was trying to escape from, the terror was problematization. He knew that he didn't need April to repeat himself, to be unchanged. She just gave him the possibility to repeat what he most wanted to, what he wanted to be the truth, what had, essentially, become the truth. Did that mean that it would do what he had hoped it would and eclipse the order of things, the so far unfruitful will to knowledge, which could possibly be a will to falsity through blind faith? No, it seemed far more probable that he was presenting himself in order to achieve a recognition, not for the sake of it.

He thought he had learnt something when he had left April, learnt something about his reasoning, about justification, not to prove or to persuade but to trust and accept. But he had just demonstrated his ignorance of the lie, a very cunning deception, the truth had been hidden in the most obvious of places, behind an hypocrisy. Everything he had confessed, and had confessed in order to uncover and expose himself to himself, had in the beginning been to attract her, but later he thought it had been a legitimate will to knowledge, only to discover that it had in fact remained a will to security. The rules all along had remained the same, the order of things was still the same, there had been no change, only a different treachery. Would such schemes continue to become increasingly elaborate?

It didn't matter. When she was around the inadequacy that was painful managed to disguise itself and that had been good enough. Now that she had gone did it mean that everything was just the same, had she not changed him in some way, if only corrupted?

'Fucking hell!' he said, blinking and rubbing his eyes and managing to look like an actor in a predictable soap opera. He knew it was a stupid idea, he even thought about it as it was happening, in disbelief, but he continued, thinking that it was what she wanted, what everyone wanted. In a soap opera nothing is ever far away, the tragic, the love affair, the righteousness, the moral, and the remote control. The truth was he couldn't be honest.

He watched April for a second, he could only see her silhouette, but could recognize its owner easily, like it was a program, a deja-vu even, a dream possibly. Only that he knew it couldn't be a dream, he knew she wasn't supposed to be there, in his doorway, coming for him, but it wasn't fantastical. It was supposed to be unreal and surprising, but it only came across as uncanny.

April got into bed with him very quickly. It crushed the surprise and he liked the fact that he hadn't the opportunity to ask her what had happened, to be surprised.

'Aren't you going to ask me what happened?' whispered April as though she might break something, in what she thought was a fragile moment.

God, he felt so abused. She could do whatever she wanted with him, come and go as she pleased. He was little more than a routine that depended on her presence or participation to exist. Her return had destroyed all his hopes of overcoming, of breaking through, of stepping out, he could say it in so many ways, but never be what he thought he might. He didn't show her any of these feelings, he kept them so well hidden so that she would not be hurt, but even more so that she would not discover his weakness, and take him for granted. At the same time he was happy and ecstatic that she was back, that she had remembered him and that he was the first thing she thought of.

He clasped her desperately to show her how much she meant to him, how much he had already missed her, to never free her again. He never answered her question because that would show her control over him, that he didn't understand the cycle he was in. His understanding was his only advantage, even if he didn't know how to escape it. The difference between him and her was that she was not in the cycle, she had demonstrated, by twice removing herself, by saying goodbye even when she didn't have to.

He waited, meditating on what he might say. Any question that he would ask might lead to the answer not being what he anticipated, that she had come back for him was the answer he wanted, but he knew that wasn't true.

A few minutes past, he dared not say a thing, barely managing, but his courage was diminishing. And then he began to question himself why she remained silent. He remembered getting upset with her because she wouldn't speak, he remembered being so worried for her, as though speech was a kind of medicine. As though saying something was like crying. He knew it was difficult for her, speaking for April was like crying in front of a huge audience. He guessed that she knew that he wanted the reason for her return to be for him, he guessed that was the reason she didn't want to say anything, because she might hurt him. She didn't want to speak of something he didn't want to hear. But wasn't *not* crying hurting oneself? Didn't it harm oneself if one didn't cry? Wasn't April hurting herself by protecting him? Why would she do such a thing? It wasn't that she needed him, it wasn't that she was too afraid to make any kind of confrontation, it wasn't to stop him from becoming upset with her and not appreciating her, was it?

He lay on his back and he feared that even if he did ask that she would never let him know. He remembered how Cherry had helped him say things, how she had helped him deal with so much. 'You know I can't read your mind,' she had said to him whenever he was confused. Now he remembered that actually he had not been confused so much as afraid to say the wrong thing, to upset her even more than she was. Had he been feeling the same as April was now?

'Do you think it is going to work between us?' he asked April.

Silence.

'Do you think its going to work between us?' he asked again.

'You always ask something intense,' whispered April.

'Why are you whispering? Are you afraid that someone might hear?'

'No.'

'You are... You're afraid that someone might hear that you can't answer my simple question... You're afraid to say anything... You're afraid that I might hear the answer, aren't you?'

It was pointless, he knew that it didn't matter how cross or upset he sounded with her, how sad or distressed, she wasn't going to give anything away. What he wanted was to prove to himself he didn't need her anymore.

'No.'

'What do you mean,' he asked, 'things *aren't* going to work?'

April nodded, and he knew that she was ashamed to be there with him now and know that in the future she would be the one to abandon him. He knew she felt ashamed, that she recognised he might feel she was using him, but she said nothing.

'Why not? Why can't it work? How can you be here with me now, and not want it to work? Don't you love me?' he cringed at the sound of his final words and maybe at the finality of them to.

'Yes, but.'

"Yes, but,' what?' He thought he could ask simple questions. Questions with "yes" or "no" answers, as he had done before with April, or had Cherry thought of it first and done the same with him, he couldn't recall. It didn't matter, April would never guess. 'Do you want me to ask you questions?'

'I don't know,' as vague as ever, but also familiar. The situation was both alien and intimate.

'Would it make it easier if I asked you questions?' He had a slight feeling that repetition had had a meagre success before, it was entrapment. Then he saw repetition as taking one step forward and two steps back, so he decided to rephrase the question. 'Do you want me to ask you questions with yes or no answers? Would that make it better?'

He surprised himself, the questions he had asked made him feel as though he wasn't the problem at all, what he was doing was lending all the responsibility to April. Maybe that was why she was finding it so difficult, maybe the things he thought she needed to say weren't so difficult, but he was portraying them as being so difficult in his approach towards them. How patronised he thought she must have felt. He knew that he was sounding as though he could say all the things that she could not, and he was sure that April was angry that she could not do what he could. She must have felt as though he was putting her on trial, for he had already decided that *he* was the victim.

He wanted to ask her something, but it had to be something he too could say if he were in her position, something in his league, and he didn't really think much of his own league at that point. But he was unwilling to sound as though he assumed too much superiority.

All he needed was another question. He had asked if she needed only "yes" or "no" questions because he thought he wouldn't have to ask many, somehow a few would be enough to get her started, and once she had begun it would be easier; that was the order anyway, that was how things had always been explained to him. He didn't believe the order anymore because it had never worked with him, but he was sure it worked with other people; no one could be like him, no way would they find things more difficult than he.

Simple answer, simple question. It must be. But it was proving impossible. Cherry could manage, as she had done so many times, but he couldn't. He thought of some questions, but he aught to think of the answers to deduce if the questions were good enough. He knew the questions could be innocent, saying anything was better than nothing, but the answers could be far from innocent. The answers could ruin everything, they could destroy him. And because he had asked the questions it would have been him who initiated the end. Was he able to take that kind of a risk? It became apparent that to ask a question, even one with a "yes" or "no" answer depended on a courage that he was without. The longer he had been with April, the more it dawned on him that he would never summon the courage that Cherry could so easily wield. Answers, so far, were by far the most important. He could ask as many questions as he liked: what he should do, who he should be, what people thought of him.

He remembered asking himself why Cherry managed to form relationships with such ease. Even if no one could speak, Cherry proved conversation only took one person, and he knew that there wasn't actually anyone speaking in his relationship with April. As long as he was worse than Cherry, he was going to feel bad. So much had been spent trying to prove to himself that he was at no disadvantage to Cherry; he would never accept that he was in this relationship with April just to prove something to himself, to Cherry. Would Cherry deduce that? Would Cherry think that it was a false relationship? Would she see right through it? Would she know how false it was, that they could not even speak to each other? Terrified that she might, a question was impossible to find.

He thought that the reason April wasn't speaking was because she was intimidated by him, by the intimacy that would, hopefully, occur. But it wasn't that at all. He hoped that she still felt that intimacy was intimidating, but he knew the silence was because he wasn't good enough, plain and simply, he was the one doing all the lying, and he was astonished by how compulsive it had become. Except that he could not, and it was necessary to do so, admit to himself that he was afraid of the intimacy.

He remembered noticing how astounded he had been when Cherry had said to him how afraid she had been to admit to herself that she could be in love. He thought his ability to admit it to himself gave him a certain kind confidence and honesty, he always felt better than her at those moments when Cherry had confessed to him, there was something she was scared of and he was not.

Fuck, he had gone against every intention, every moral that he had ever had. What he thought he had been doing was completely innocent, but every time he had fallen in love or been with someone was because he could not do without. He had to be with someone because his survival was impossible without someone else. He wasn't afraid of intimacy for the simple reason that he needed to believe that he wasn't afraid. He didn't even have the courage to be sincere with himself to accept that he was afraid, perhaps even April could do that, she had made clear that fear prevented her from so much, just not in so many words, at least she hadn't denied.

He was afraid of intimacy, that was why he was thinking of the answers that April might give, rather than thinking of the questions, that was why he couldn't say things were over between them, that was why he felt worse than Cherry, that was why he was so hopelessly stuck. Fear of intimacy and fear of solitude.

He felt that the truth came as he thought it might, when he was alone, decidedly. He felt as though he was going over the motions of a conclusion, that he had been fooling himself about being able, when April and he had been together, perhaps that was why she had been silent; there were things about her that had escaped him. Certainly he had thought that he could help her, but he was glad that he had realized, albeit through failure, that he could not. Ironically it seemed realization of inadequacy was something April had given him, like it was something he should feel grateful for, and he did. He gave her more benefit than he had given anyone before, he wouldn't have come this far without her. It wasn't that she was traumatized, rather he was incapable of helping her, he wasn't good enough, even worse was that he had taken so long to realize, the atrocity of putting her through so much, for this, his own end. What a hypocrite he had been blaming her, if only in his mind, that she was so selfish, when all had only served his own ends.

For five days scenarios were repeated, he didn't know if it was pleasurable or not, there didn't seem to be an end. He thought that because he had seduced her that would mean that he could seduce more then her desire, that he could conjure in her such desire that she would be addicted. He never once thought that she might know what he was doing, that someone might have done the same to her before. Was there anything original about it? How tired he felt.

'You make a funny noise at night,' said April.

'What like? Am I saying something?'

'No.'

'I'm grinding my teeth, I know.'

'Yeah.'

'It's really bad, I know,' demonstrating it and imagining his teeth shattering under the pressure.

He had done it all his life, sometimes more, sometimes less. It even happened during the day. He would be walking, thinking, and he would find his face tightly clenched, his teeth forced together in an unprisable clasp, as if he was trying to keep things from getting in, intrusion. He even had to train himself not to, making a conscious effort to separate his jaws in a vacant face only to find it clenching after saying something, it caught him off guard for days at a time. He had been clenching his teeth for five days.

What would Thomas have done in his position? He would have clenched his teeth on April's love handles and not let go until there was nothing left for her to give. The problem was that he still thought that because she was holding back from him that there was still something that she could give or share. He was actually the one who had dried up into a void, become nothing, saying the exact same things or nothings when she left. In a way it was a last desperate attempt to become something or at least an illusion of something that she might be able to see.

Chapter 9

He looked Cherry as closely in the eye as the darkness would allow. She was smiling at him and he could see that she was fully amused by what had happened to him while he was away. He had written everything to her, telling was so compulsive, it couldn't be helped. He thought about how strange it was to be writing such things to an exgirlfriend, he thought about what others might think, what April might think, but their judgments weren't enough. He had such an urge to show Cherry that he could fall in love, that it was possible for him to have a good time, a good time that was made all the more significant by the fact that Cherry had not shared it. Things could sound as though he had enjoyed himself so much more than Cherry had; he didn't have to lie so much as to leave things out.

The more he spoke to Cherry about his time away the more she looked interested. It didn't matter if she only wanted to hear that he had enjoyed himself, to him any interest at all, whether it was just in what he was saying, he felt it was in him. Cherry had not shown that much interest, that much enthusiasm, in so long, it was so nourishing. All she had done before was repeatedly say that she wanted him to be happy, but he never believed her. The more in love he said he was the more Cherry smiled and laughed in her own particular cackle that he could distinguish from any sound, he had hated going out with her and hearing her laugh because someone else had made her do so.

His plane had arrived in the early hours of the morning and he had made his way back through the darkness, on buses that had become more familiar through habit, or rather less familiar through the unawareness that habit brings. The buses were meant to eliminate the time it took for the sun to rise, but they didn't.

The house was unhealthily cold and he could have sworn it was meant to look different to how he had left it. He didn't know if it was possible to remember exactly where things were after so long, but he was sure that those magazines were the ones that he had left on the kitchen table. The fridge was not as empty as he thought it might have been. He was hungry, nothing spoke to him, or seduced him, things wanted to make him weak. He was glad to be inside though. London was so much easier to categorize and criticize, to sweep aside in its superficiality. But with this superficiality came a kind of aggressiveness, the kind one might have to become in order to deal with harshness, greed. He might have been happy to notice things like that hadn't they made him feel vulnerable, more vulnerable than before, or was it just that he was noticing things more and vulnerability was the price he had to pay for such awareness? Was the choice one of strength and ignorance or weakness and awareness? He was confident, or rather the more confident he became that he was shrinking the more scared he was. Did even thinking of these kinds of questions make him weak?

He remembered his graduation day. He never really wanted to go, but thought that he should at least send his gran a picture of him in his gown and board for all that she had given him in support. His mother had gone with him to the ceremony to take a video so that they could show Gran. It had been fine, he hadn't stayed around for drinks with anyone else from his college because of his mother. Afterwards they had walked around town for a little while, he followed her around in his suit which he was wearing for the first time. The suit made him feel so skinny, that was one thing he hated, looking skinny, it was so far away from the image he wanted to present, of being a strong man.

His mother had stepped into a shop and he had tried to follow, but had stepped in front of someone. They tutted and, for reasons he couldn't define, he tutted back. He heard swearing coming from behind him and just as he was turning around, a man head butted him in the face and then started screaming in it, asking if he wanted a fight. He had become aware of his mother watching all this going on. It was quite amazing how he had managed to calm the guy down, how he had avoided being beaten up. He knew afterwards, when he was left standing there, his legs shaking, that he would never have been able to put up a fight, it didn't matter how big or small the opponent was, he would only ever be able to try and defend himself. From that point on he never understood violence, however he came into contact with it, he always felt sick. He thought how embarrassing he must have looked to his mother, he followed her around the shop they had originally wanted to go into and he noticed the guy's sweat all over his face, he tried to wipe it away, but it was no use, the smell lingered on him for the rest of the day. The smell of old, fat greasy man. It was strange how dirty the smell of another persons sweat made him feel, it was as if all the dirt on the street, on the ground, was seeping through his skin and entering his stomach and then coming up with indigestion and he could taste it. The shit was trying to get out of his eyes and he had to try desperately to stop crying, to stop his eyes stinging. It was the worst day, at least one of the most embarrassing.

As he had climbed the stairs to bed, he put his hands in exactly the same places as he had always done. He had watched other people falling into such habits, he was even interested in the effects, but he was too tired to notice anything now. If he thought about being back it took a lot off his mind, but it left him slightly empty, even bored already. All that had changed, emptiness had been superseded by the sound of Cherry coming back from her night shift. Cherry ran up the stairs, that was how much attention she was going to give him, that was how important he was to her.

He kept talking and he wondered how long it was going to be until she would tell him to stop showing off. He could make her laugh again and there was none of the petty criticism that he was used to giving her, right then he didn't have to make what he had done while he was away sound more intriguing than anything she might have done. By the way he was speaking, it sounded as though he cared little for her experience, he just kept talking about himself, there was a chance that he might have shown interest in Cherry had she said something that would surprise him enough for him not to be able to find something that was more extreme, more interesting, more shocking, better, to interrupt her with, to destroy.

Cherry had to have been influenced into believing that he was far more infatuated with April than herself when she felt secure enough to fall asleep right there in the bed with him. She must have thought he and Cherry were just friends, maybe he had made her think in that way, but he didn't know if it was the lack of criticism or the lack of dependence on her that made the difference.

He woke up and it was beginning to get light, Cherry was still sleeping. He couldn't sleep anymore, nothing worked. Boredom took over, all he really wanted to do was tell Cherry how great he was, so that maybe when she did find out some of the things that he hated that had happened to him she would not be so disappointed.

He persuaded himself that Cherry admired him enough. He had told her how in love he was with April, but now he was pulling Cherry's panties to one side, they weren't particularly sexy, the kind a girl wears and says that it is for comfort and that they don't care what they look like. He wasn't really thinking how she might react when she woke up, and there was no way that she was going to stay asleep, but the idea was to manage for as long as possible while she was asleep and then deal with the rest later. Cherry just wasn't lying in the right position to slip inside her, so he got on top. He was never really confident when it came to the female sex, he didn't know if he was hurting them when he touched them or if it felt nice, or how to move his tongue, or even where the clitoris was. He had got into the habit of saying that he didn't know where the clitoris was, it was true, but to April it sounded like a joke, she never believed him however much he would say it was true. It made him feel good that someone thought he knew something that he didn't, someone actually thought he was much better at sex than he actually was. It had been really hard to take when Cherry had made it very clear that she had found men that were better at love than he was, he knew that it shouldn't be important, "love is important", people would say. He thought a person needs exceptional self confidence to really believe. Was it the same kind of confidence that was lost when it was sacrificed for awareness, the kind he had become aware of losing on his return?

He had no justification, he thought he was in love with someone else, and despised people, especially Cherry, for having sex with people that they were not in love with. He didn't think that he was any better at making love than before, he didn't think that she was going to fall in love with him again, nothing. Perhaps things had changed so much that by fucking her now he could declare some new found independence.

As he lay on top of her and slid carefully up and down, he

wondered if she was awake or not, if her panties were far enough to the right. He thought she was awake, maybe that was a better sign than her being asleep, maybe she didn't mind. He wasn't inside her yet, she was a little too dry, but he liked the need to apply a little pressure, to feel a little pain, that was the most sexy thing he could think of, he thought that once he was inside her everything would be alright, Cherry would continue to make love even if afterwards she would hate herself for doing it.

But it didn't quite work. He raised himself a little, spat in his hand, wiped it on his dick and then lowered himself again, easily sliding inside her. It was true what they said about men, that men didn't like foreplay, but what they also said about men only wanting to come, that was wrong. What he wanted to do was remain laying there, perhaps forever, feeling warmth, feeling. Entering was meant to be the beginning of making love and the exit was meant to be the end, yet it wasn't like that at all, he could hardly think of anything else, entering was just a void, he couldn't even think about thinking further, there existed no future. It was the most wonderful feeling in the world, and it was all taken away by the expectation of performance.

He used to make love like that with Cherry, softly, hardly moving, he thought that was what love was. When he had first met her, their first night together they had made love, and he had done what he thought was appropriate, what he had done for years with other girlfriends. But, later Cherry would joke about how soft he was, that she couldn't believe it, that she hadn't dared to move because she thought something was emotionally wrong with him. She always reminded him of how he had stopped and whispered in her ear that he had come, she thought that was "so sweet". Those words destroyed everything, maybe they didn't destroy what he thought making love was meant to be, but it ruined any perception that it was what women wanted.

There was just no way that he could stay still. If Cherry wasn't going to tell her friends later about how weird it had been that he just lay on top of her, then she was at least going to think that of him, or he was going to feel ashamed anyway. It was like he wanted to be with someone, for certain reasons, but didn't for others. He wanted to show that he was a changed person and that meant completely severing any ties to the past, Cherry, their first day, his sentimental love making, all of it.

He started moving. He felt so clumsy. But he was determined. Cherry was all women, she epitomized exactly what a woman was and what they wanted, if he could just hope to satisfy her then he would not be so afraid. This kind of exhaustive movement was not what he thought was good sex, or sexually good, but she never made many sounds when he made love to her. He wanted to hear her making the sounds he knew other men had heard, to be able was part of the change that being away and April had given him.

In a way he was relieved when he came, normally he would feel terrible, it was one thing that put him off making love, continually having to slow or stop every two or three minutes to stop himself from coming, and knowing that Cherry really wanted to go on with the same kind of movement for ages. He always wondered how it could be different for other men, how he had been inflicted with premature ejaculation, what would love making be like otherwise? Relief came with not having to make those horrid movements any longer.

Cherry opened her eyes when he pulled out and lay beside her. She didn't say anything, neither did her face, it didn't change at all, it only expressed her tiredness.

He had a few moments to wonder why he hated those strong sexual movements so much, to worry why he detested them so much. Maybe they were really sexy, that was why they made him come so quickly. Maybe he hated them because they made him come so quickly and he had made up some ulterior motive for hating them just so that he didn't have to encounter his inadequacy. He hated those fucking absurd movements because others could do them and he couldn't. He even hated watching them on television, even on a porno, or whenever someone would comment on them favourably. It was the kind of worry that he would never be able to do anything about, like his dandruff or having to copy to make anything up; or what about his verukas on his feet that he would keep a secret by never showing his feet to anyone, and if he had to then he would find an uncomfortable way to hide the soles. They were just things that he knew other people would find disgusting, so he didn't want to show them, sometimes he would forget about them as well, but never for long enough. He sometimes thought that other people had secrets too, that they had something that they were hiding from everyone, little defects that they were ashamed of. Then he fell asleep as quickly as she did, her face turned away from his, distancing.

'Please don't eat that in front of me,' was the first thing Cherry said to him the next day.

'What?' He had heard what she had said, but it was so different from what he had expected, the words had almost been morphed into the words he was sure he was going to hear, it was like saying something and thinking of another word at the same time and mixing them up together and not being able to do anything about it.

'What?' he asked in vain after receiving no acknowledgement.

Cherry stared into space, at particularly nothing, he knew that meant that she was making clear that she wasn't going to say anything because, ironically, he had always done the same. He didn't want to press her on it, he wanted to forget, or wanted her to forget, and speaking about the night before was only going to prolong its presence.

He occupied himself for a while, in his room, trying to change things, to make absolutely sure that he had changed himself. It wasn't necessary for him to talk to Cherry anymore, he didn't need her, or anyone.

'Where have you been?' he asked when he decided to give Cherry some recognition, but only enough to actually let her know that he was there and not the other way round.

'To the GP's,' said Cherry bluntly, still not looking at him.

'Oh,' understated, 'what for?'

'The morning after pill,' she said without the expected resentment.

'But you,' abbreviating because of unsureness. What was he really going to say? Nothing worthy came to mind. He could run through the motions, explain the story to himself, really, he knew the story from beginning to end, no one needed to tell him. Silence might bring a pretence of innocence. He could show the precise opposite, his complete confidence, but his thoughts lacked enough clarity. Clarity depended on hindsight, of which he suffered so extensively.

He didn't need Cherry to say that she felt terrible, he had come to recognize all of her emotional states instantaneously. Most of the time he couldn't see anything through his own guilt, but he knew he had to do something, she was going to speak and he wanted to act before she got the chance. The urge for a kind of competition undermined all his thoughts, bigger, better, faster. Faster. Could he manage innovation before she asked, would that improve circumstances, would that, ultimately, bring him to the origin? Did his immediate blindness exceed that of the night before?

Suddenly, everything was different, cereal wasn't cereal anymore, nor was toast, it was all guilt. Breakfast wasn't for hunger, it wasn't for routine either, it was to avoid, to avoid Cherry and the GP. He didn't want to do anything, he didn't want to move from the spot because there wasn't anything he could do to ameliorate. He was going to remain within Cherry's view, that would demonstrate that he wasn't avoiding anything, that would be saying that he did fuck her without protection the night before. Admission, was good. He was frozen, but he could persuade himself that it was for good reason, not loss.

The fact that he wasn't moving was making him cold, mostly his toes and fingers. The instance called for silence, looking at the floor; he felt his throat needed clearing, but he wouldn't dare, and he felt it worsening until he needed to cough. He held the cough back until it was of no use and he let out almost without realizing it was coming, it took him by such surprise that he had been unable to keep the saliva inside. Mucous and saliva shot out and he just managed to catch it in his hand and somehow divert attention from himself rather badly, he then sucked it off his hand because he didn't know what else to do with it.

He sat down on the couch next to Cherry and asked if there was anything she wanted. Cherry didn't reply. He continued with his silence, but it felt worse than if she would have been blaming him. The silence that the cough had broken had returned and the longer it stayed the more important something had to be to break it. Another cough was on the way, for some reason he dared not or even move at all, not even diverting his eyes from Cherry. He knew that looking at someone directly was perceived as responsible, it didn't matter that Cherry probably hadn't noticed, or didn't care, or didn't think he was a responsible person. He could feel his throat getting more and more itchy. He had to concentrate intently to stop himself from erupting, he could feel his eyes starting to water. What, he wondered, would happen if Cherry thought he was crying?

Years ago, when he split up with his first girlfriend, he had not known what to do. He hadn't known what was wrong with himself. When he saw her he only wanted her attention, but she wouldn't give it to him unless something was wrong, so he would ask her if he could talk to her and make something up, but she caught on after a while, suspecting that nothing was wrong other than him feeling sorry for himself, and she would refuse to talk to him in private. Then he tried to throw something a little more earnest at her so she could not avoid, it came to a point where he had to cry to get her attention, but crying was an obstacle because he couldn't, ever. Sometimes he would want to cry for not being able. He would catch his exgirlfriend and sit with her in silence, focusing his eyes on something in the distance, anything, making sure that she would not notice that he wasn't blinking. He would hold his eyes open for as long as possible until they filled with tears, if that didn't work then he had discovered a way of yawning without actually showing any signs of doing so, a kind of half yawn, which would actually give him the feeling he would get for the first few seconds when he actually was crying. Then he would look at her directly and make something up that was wrong with her and that wasn't resolvable. He would never have forgiven her if she would have said that he just loved to make problems that weren't solvable, but she would have been right, all the problems that he made up didn't have a solution. What he wanted was time with her and the problems, if only briefly, did get solved for as long as he could pretend to cry. He never really felt guilty about pretending to do something like that because he never shed any real tears and he thought what he was doing was in some way making up for that.

As a couple of tears started, he made a few sighs in emphasis. He knew he had caught Cherry's attention, but she wasn't looking at him or asking what was wrong. The situation lasted long enough for him to think about what had really happened. Cherry might have been pregnant.

Cherry finally spoke and she sounded sure that she had been pregnant, that he had made her pregnant. They had something like an argument about whose fault it was, if Cherry had wanted sex or not, why she had allowed him inside her; he knew it was all pointless, she had let him in because she could, he had fucked her because he was still in love with her, but unwilling to admit.

Paramount was that he had made her pregnant and using his few tears he persuaded her that it made him think of his own fatherless life. After all he could have been a father. Having a father, or rather, not having a father was something that he never let himself dwell on for too long, people asked him about it, how it was not to have a figure to rely on, but he always replied that because he had never had one, he had nothing to compare it to. He knew that he was deflecting things, making someone else feel sorry for him, when actually he should be feeling sorry for what he had done.

The truth was he dreamt of apologising, and it made it even more difficult to stop feeling sorry for himself, he needed someone to tell him that everything would be alright, that what he had done was not as bad as he thought. If Cherry would ask him questions about his father right then and there, he would feel as though he hadn't done anything wrong. He would even go a step further and say that he wanted her to be pregnant, he wanted a father. Anything extreme and emotional could be turned the right way, could be used to advantage, to get Cherry to feel sorry for him and not the other way round. Everything he had done he could, if he really wanted, turn into something he did because he had been hurt, or because he had felt neglected. He had done things because he needed support, they weren't bad, they were things that were trying to say that he needed help. The more he played on it the more he did think about his father, that he didn't even really know his name, had never got praise from anyone like a father, someone that really counted, he had never been shown what responsibilities were.

He told Cherry that he didn't even know his father's name, it was even worse that he could only say that he thought it was Peter. How pathetic it must have sounded to be unsure of a name that was so important. He had nothing, and he was ignoble. Could one have less, perhaps prison was less than nothing, perhaps he was imprisoned in some way? Slowly he began to forget why he had embarked on such deception and started to really cry. Family, parents, children, babies, all started to become mixed up, if he had the opportunity to become a father, it would remind him that he was fatherless. Lapse of remission.

'I want to ask my mother what my father's name is, I want to be sure, I hate not being absolutely sure,' he said, the words interrupted by deep sighs that made him feel like a child. 'I would like to know what he looks like, if he is anything like me,' he was beginning to sound like he was asking Cherry things, treating her like his mother. 'What should I do? I could try and find him, but I'm so shit I probably wouldn't be able to, I don't even know where to start? When I watch soap operas, I never understand why it's such a cliché story, children trying to find their parents, I don't feel like doing the same because that would make my life a cliché. How could my father do that to me? How could he just leave me on my own? Does he not even wonder about me? Does he never think about how I am doing?' he began to wonder if he could make the irresponsible thing that he had done sound good, or at least not too bad, in comparison to what his father had done. If that didn't succeed, then at least it might make the fact that Cherry had had to take the morning after pill sound insignificant in comparison with his life without a father. Gulping and interruptive sighs began to annoy him, he couldn't quite say anything without having to repeat it several times to make sure that Cherry had understood, the difficulty of repetition.

Chapter *10*

April and he had been keeping their relationship going on the telephone. She would never call him, but he was persuaded that her disregard was due to business and lack of time. He knew that she was still living with her boyfriend and he kept asking her why, she would say that he was looking for a flat, but it was hard to find. He asked if they had been sleeping together since she had been back and she said they hadn't. He told her what a terrible time he had after she had left him and that he could only think of returning and being with her.

When Cherry asked him how things were going with April, he always felt good and would say so, he never really felt alone, single. April never tried to put him off on the phone and would still say that she loved him when they said goodbye. He knew that he was making her boyfriend jealous every time he called her, sometimes her boyfriend would even pick the phone up, then he would hear from April how her boyfriend had left the house in a hurry. Jokes would be made to other people about what a wild situation it was, perhaps what was most important was that it was something, something to talk about, to be involved in, and that was what he thought he was, involved.

Cherry would always tell him to be careful, she would say that she didn't like April, that April was not taking care of him. He would always question her motives for asking such things, he would ask if she was just jealous, believing she had to be, but she would say no, that she was only worried about him. She would ask if April's boyfriend had moved out yet and he would tell her that would happen as soon as possible. Every now and then Cherry would also ask if April was going to come and visit for a while. The truth was that April had been continually putting it off; tickets couldn't be got, work had to be done. Then April decided on a date and he was so happy, how sure he was that things were going to work. The only person that he really wanted to tell was Cherry, it would prove so much to her, his independence and all that came with it, responsibility, personal satisfaction, all the things that Cherry had been happy for him to have but obviously doubted from the moment he had sex with her when he got back. Grandad always used to say that the things that he would buy with his own money that he had worked for, he would treasure far more than anything he was given.

They fell on to their friends bed, they had gone over to attend a barbecue, but left everyone to be alone. He kissed Cherry, he noticed how hard their kissing had become, her roughness meant excitement. The sun was coming in through the window and landing on his back, someone came in and saw them, pulled an embarrassed smile and then left. How confident he felt, he didn't really know what was happening between him and Cherry. He could only compare it to times when they were together, when they would go for a few days without sleeping together and then they would go through a period where it was as if they couldn't get enough of each other. The difference was that now the thought of having sex with her would never make him feel tired, he had the energy to do anything, nothing would put him off, he didn't think about much else.

If other people were around him and Cherry, then he would always make it look as though things were formally over and that they could still get on like mature friends, but he wanted even the greatest sceptics converted, so he started making it look as though he didn't like her and he started to feel that way as well. If she was ever enthusiastic about something he would always play whatever it was down, trying to show her that what she was excited about was nothing. He always expected her to get upset with him and tell him to be a little happier for her, but she never did. If she had, his happiness for her wouldn't have lasted long, he was beginning to hate her. It wasn't simple, he wouldn't have been able to describe, to anyone, exactly what it was because so many things aggravated him, that made him want to lash out at her. He would get angry enough sometimes to throw things, he even knocked a saucepan full of boiling potatoes in her direction once. He wanted to beat her so that she would take more notice of him. He pictured grabbing her by the neck and pushing her up against the wall and telling her to do as he said because recently she had not respected any of his wishes. It wasn't that he thought he wanted to have control over her, he wasn't that angry, just that he was upset and thought that she wasn't even noticing him and he was tired of feeling like he was being walked over. He couldn't work out if she was doing less of what he asked because they weren't together, or if she was doing less because she wanted to make him feel insignificant. What he had pictured had become a little bit of an obsession and one day when she walked into the room he asked her to get out. She refused and without even thinking or hardly being provoked, he tried to grab her by the throat, but he was stopped by her hands. He didn't want to make a fool of himself by completely failing what he had set out to do, so he tried to cover up the failure by pretending that he hadn't really been planning anything like that at all. He tried to get his hands free enough to get hold of her neck, but he couldn't, so he ended up waving his and her arms around stupidly. Eventually he did get her against the wall, at which point he wanted to say she should pay some respect, but before he got the chance she made him feel stupid by asking him what he was trying to achieve. He told her that he didn't know and let her go, not that he really had any hold of her.

He then ran out to Nathan's house, where he wanted to pretend that he had a real friend whom he could confide in for the first time. Nathan was willing to listen, but it took a long time for him to say anything, when he did, he told Nathan what had happened and tried to reassure himself that what he had done was not bad. He didn't explain that he had been thinking about it for days, planning to grab her by the neck. He was in a dilemma because, in a way, he wanted to be in a position where Nathan might say that what he had done was not bad, on the other hand he also wanted to have done something bad and get sympathy for doing such an awful deed, confused as to whether he would get more sympathy for doing something not so bad, as opposed to something terrible. Nathan didn't really give him either, only saying how he had hit his girlfriend some years ago and he felt really bad about it. He kept telling Nathan how bad he felt and that he never thought he could do anything like that. He thought he might cry for a second and then he asked if he could sleep over at Nathan's, so as to avoid seeing Cherry at least for a night, he thought that this suggestion might lend some severity to the situation. The other way he tried to give it a serious edge was by saying that he needed fresh air, when actually he was quite cold. When Nathan agreed they went out to the park, he thought he looked desperate and that he was someone to worry about, but Nathan didn't say anything.

When he got home the next morning he didn't say anything to Cherry, he was waiting for her to be angry with him, instead he was greeted with questions of worry. Cherry asked him where he had been all night, and that she had called people asking where he was. He should have been happy except now other people knew what had happened, that was something he hadn't been planning for days, how she was going to tell people what he had done to her. Not even Cherry took what he thought was an immoral gesture, very seriously. He was the one who was supposed to be worried about her, not the other way around, the only concern she should have, if any, was for his humanity.

So it was strange that when he was alone with her he could also be needing her so desperately, that things could just change from contempt to lust. Why was it that she was allowing him make love to her again after all he had done to her? Yes, he did admit to himself that he had been horrid, but only to himself, as far as anyone else was concerned with his opinion, everything he had done to her was her own fault, she was in the wrong, she had done something to him, she had hurt him.

'We better not do that again,' said Cherry, getting dressed, as though she didn't really want to admit that they had sex.

'Why?'

'Because I don't think it's very good, for us, for you.'

There they were, those magic words again, those words that brought everything to bear on him. If he was not the one that was responsible for doing the damage, then he was the one being damaged. He was tired of hearing them, he was tired of telling himself them.

'I don't want you to think that we are going to get back together again,' continued Cherry.

'Why do we still make love then, why do you have sex with me?'

'I hate to say it, but it's because I can, because I know that you are good in bed, you know what I like. I was a little disappointed when I found out how much you were in love with April. I wanted to know if I could still seduce you. I wanted to know if you would still be attracted to me even if you were in love with someone else. I wanted power. I didn't feel sexy any longer when I wasn't sure that you desired me or not.'

'All this time I didn't think that you had feelings for me. You think that I am stupid. I can take care of myself. I wish you would stop talking to me as though you had complete power over me, taking care of me as though I am useless. You know, it feels like you are trying to control me.'

'Look, it's obvious that we can't live together, I was just fooling myself that we could be friends. Someone told me about a room that was going, I think I can move into that, I'll find out tomorrow.'

'I hate you! All this time I think I am the one fucking up, I am the one taking the guilt for these things happening. Yeah, it's nice that you say you are sorry to me, but Cherry, you make me feel like nothing, like you can use me as you like, when you like, do you know how that makes me feel?' he had to say such things, he had such an urge to, but at the same time he really didn't want to. He wanted to be portrayed as the victim, but that wasn't going to make him into the person that he so wanted to be. It was so difficult to have to beg for an apology, for help, for recognition. In a way he would rather be the one inflicting the pain on someone, then he wouldn't have to suffer, and suffer when he had to ask for the suffering to be recognised.

Chapter *11*

Cherry had been gone for a few weeks and he didn't really feel as alone as she had implied he would. He had helped Cherry move all her stuff, in a way he had helped her because he thought that she had moved because of him, because it was so hard for him to take all the things that she did, or more importantly, all the things that he thought she might do. He felt a little guilty, but wouldn't admit that she was doing him a favour; what he would do was find an excuse that made him more eligible to the house then she was, after all he had more stuff than she did. But the truth was that he couldn't move out, he didn't know how, where to begin, what to do, moreover he couldn't leave Cherry.

April was coming soon and that was all he could think about, being lonely as Cherry had worried about had not come to mind, only being a little bored. There wasn't anything to do, of course there were things to be done, always, but not that he wanted to do by himself.

Nobody would have been told if he was lonely or not, it would have been difficult for him to accept it himself. He wondered how people actually told one another, if there was someone close enough to tell about being lonely then you couldn't really be lonely. If you were really telling someone, really conveying what you were feeling then you couldn't really be alone, it might even be that in those moments, of pure unsupplemented communication, that aloneness disappeared and only in those moments. Maybe it was something that only happened in hindsight, people would only say they had been lonely, not that they were so in the present. Maybe only memories were lonely, maybe because they couldn't really be shared. It seemed that sharing was lonely, not being able to do it, that is, not being able to share, that would cut one off from the rest of the world. Worst would be not being able to share lonely memories, or maybe memories only became lonely if they were unshareable. Share-ability, he thought, was what determined loneliness. And memories would be more difficult to share if they were lonely, and that would make them more lonely, and it would continue until nothing was shared and the only memory's one had were lonely. Nobody ever witnessed anyone's loneliness unless it was their own, it was something so common, yet unshareable, made more so by its abjectness.

He never felt the need to speak about loneliness, but he could be confusing need with ability, which would be an easy kind of mistake to make, and one that he assumed many people, he didn't know, made. But, most importantly, he didn't like talking about being lonely because that meant that he was a lonely person, if it wasn't a problem then nobody needed to talk about it. This way of maintaining oneself only became a problem the day that he got the letter from April, it wasn't the letter that really brought it home.

It was the same day that he had received the letter. He was walking home, in the distance, before he turned right down the small alley which he used for a short cut, he saw what looked like a bright blue jacket in the middle of the wide sidewalk. He was going to turn right and forget about it, but then he wondered what it was doing there, he had the strangest feeling that he could just make out a person inside the jacket, but he wasn't sure because it would be strange to be lying down on the street.

He turned down the alley with a clear picture of what he had left on the street. When he got to the end, he wished to see what it was. He decided that he wasn't going to do anything, just look, the decision was very clear, nothing more than look. As he walked closer, he realized that it was a person after all, it was a man, who wasn't sleeping, nor did he look ill, in fact he couldn't find an explanation for why the man was lying down like that.

'I'm going to die,' said the man looking directly at him, straight in his eyes, 'I'm going to die.'

What the man had said didn't feel shocking at all, more reasonable, and the longer he looked down at the half jacket half man and looked around, the more reasonable a kind of thing it would be to say. He stood watching, not really knowing if he should be disgusted or if he should take pity, there were things that he needed, to get inside, for example, to get warm, not to be out there with the jacket.

The sky was very low, not quite foggy, but verging on a mist, the visibility similar because of the soft rain that was falling vertically, not because it was very windy, but because the drops were so light they could hardly be felt on the face or hands. The rain represented the entire scene, the whole day. Everything could be seen, but not felt. The greyness could not be felt, neither did any of the passers by feel anything for the man and his lonely audience, their cars just drove by one after another as though they hadn't seen anything at all, the only sound that came from them was the kind of sound tyres make on a slightly wet road, the kind that makes them seem hollow, not solid, futuristic. It was empty, there were no other pedestrians because nobody wanted to be out on a day like that, the weather was not too bad, but it was very deceptive. One could have mistaken the scene, he was beginning to lose any sensation, for the cold, for being able to tell exactly what was going on, for death, for empathy, for recognition that he was actually there, not just watching, where do the boundaries between watching and awareness meet? Where do they end? Had they reached the end for him?

'I'm going to die,' said the man for the last time before he shut his eyes.

The man had frozen him.

'Call the ambulance,' he thought, 'go home, get warm. Wait around, continue to watch, see if he dies. Go home and ring the ambulance, even though home is further than the phone box. Don't do anything at all. Don't move. Lay down, find out what it is like for this person. I have everything and this guy doesn't have a thing, he is going to die on the street. What would that be like? Would I still see him tomorrow, would he still be here, the cars going past, would they be the same cars going past on their way back or to work? Am I stupid for wondering what to do? Am I a bad person? What kind of morals do I have? This guy never did anything for me, if I was on the street, would he take any kind of care, anything at all? Why does nobody else come to help? We aren't that dissimilar. My house feels a bit like this, I hate home, it's as cold as outside. This is like my home, nobody looks, it's as if there are walls around us, my home is just as invisible. Wait a second, why the fuck am I invisible? Or is it that the people see me, but not this other guy? What difference would it make to anyone if this kind of person dies? Nobody has noticed so far, he is as good as dead now, but he isn't. Would anyone notice if I died? Would anyone care?'

It was a little too much to bare, having no sensation. Look at the effect no sensation has, it's even more difficult to deal with. He had to turn away. Was there anything to turn to? As he turned away, he forgot about the jacket man, it was like he hadn't experienced anything at all. He hated when Cherry said someone else had taught her something new, when actually he knew very well he had done the same with her or taught her exactly the same thing, it felt like he had not existed at all, like they had never been together, if she didn't remember it then perhaps it hadn't happened. But this experience was a little different, he remembered what had happened, that he had seen a guy on the street, but he didn't really know what he felt about it, there weren't any emotions attached to it. He almost felt like turning around to make sure that the jacket man was still there, to make sure that it was serious, serious enough not to forget about. In a way he wanted the jacket man to be there, still.

After a few metres, he could remember perfectly; the greyness, the stillness, the silence, the colour of the man's jacket, but he couldn't remember if there was a person, if there was a person lying on the street or if it was only a jacket. He couldn't remember what colour the eyes were meant to be or what colour the hair was meant to be. And there was meant to be someone, who's characteristics would distinguish them from someone else, but none could be remembered; like a void that was supposed to be inhabited. The further he walked the more it was like trying to build something which the elements so easily eroded, a conquest against nature.

At that moment April's letter became significant, of course it had upset him when he had opened it, but it wasn't what it said that was so pitiful, it was thinking about what he was going to do now that he had read it.

'*My beauty*,' April had scribbled to him on a shitty piece of lined paper and sent in a beautiful red envelope, '*sorry, but I can't come to see you. Not now, not ever. I really love you and it is difficult for me to be saying this, you have learnt how difficult it is for me to hurt you. I didn't want to, ever, but you at least taught me to be a little compassionate, and I think that you, unlike me, would rather know the truth than live in a lie. You once told me that if I would lie to you and leave it for a long time that you would be in love with the lie and not me. Well, I hope that you were in love with me at one point at least, otherwise I am sorry that I wasted your time, but not everything I said was a lie. I would like you to know that there was a point where you really grabbed and pulled every string in me that I wanted/needed to be pulled, as though you knew exactly what I wanted, maybe I was too scared of having everything, maybe wanting is what keeps me going, but when you said to me that you wanted my children and to get married, I almost fell for you, but I knew that it was too good, and that you were joking. I really do love you. Please don't call because I am still living with my boyfriend and it really hurts him if he picks up the phone. Love April.'*

It was so sad for him that she really had wanted the family thing, and that she almost had done it. He had known that she was yearning to have children and that when she saw a child she was driven a little crazy, but it was never his motive for saying those things to her. It was just so sad that she was preventing two people that wanted the same things from meeting each other and being together.

What he realized was that without the prospect of April coming he hadn't anything to do. Everything had been pinned on her. Nobody had lied to him before, not like that, not deliberately. What a fool he had been to think that no one could actually lie to him, he had never even thought about it. He had heard other people talking about being lied to, other people had even suggested that April might be lying. Now he realized why he hadn't believed anyone, what they had said didn't even stay in his memory for very long, only a feeling of people's general mistrust, but he had to trust her, how could he believe, love, someone that lied, that was dishonest, that cheated. April was a good person, he always fell in love with women that were far better than he was. If April had been so dishonest, then what did that make of him, how crap would that make him, did he lie? Obviously to himself. Lying to oneself was far worse than lying to someone else, he had thought, in fact he had said that lying to others was lying to oneself. Others would become friends with your lie and then you would think that they were your friends, tell yourself that they were your friends, when actually they weren't. A lie would take friendship away, even if the person lied to didn't know they were being deceived, even if they hadn't ended the friendship, the liar had, a long time ago. It was also almost impossible for the liar to end a fake life, the lie dominated everything, it sunk the person so deep that they would have to make lies in order to sustain the first, and then substitute the sustaining lie for another and another, until at one point it didn't really feel like deceiving any more, and there would be no way out, no escape, no end, definitely no reversal.

That was one thing that a liar usually couldn't understand, there is no reversal, no way of making a lie into a truth. The truth couldn't just be told in order to end the lie, salvation did not come by telling the truth. Not that once someone was a liar then they would always be liars, but that salvation was not the reason for being honest. He too didn't know what the reason for honesty was. It definitely didn't have anything to do with being fair to other people, they wouldn't know the difference. No, it was about being honest with oneself, not that there was an absolute truth, or anything like that, but it was something to do with being able to choose. Choice was eliminated once lies were involved. So far he hadn't had a choice.

"Not now, not ever," "I'm going to die," "not now, not ever," the words kept repeating in his head. The thought of death arose. What would it be like to be alive forever and be alone always? What would it be like to always be alone? 'Oh, my god.' He realized that he had been alone forever, all the time that he knew, alone. Perhaps the difference between that thing on the street and him was not that significant. Did people mistake him for a thing, a jacket, something covering, protecting from elements? Could he bear the struggle of finding someone else now that April had rejected him? Why had she? Because he was not good enough, he thought, because he hadn't done enough for her.

No one was going to answer his questions for him, they might tell him something, they might reply, but in the end he would have to decide whether or not to acknowledge their reply, they were in the same position as him, weren't they?

He noticed how slowly he was walking. The ground was moving very quickly past his feet and leaving him. He had been looking at the floor all the way and couldn't look up because it somehow stung his eyes. The light might have been responsible, but it wasn't actually that bright. It could be that he hadn't been out for a long time, the air inside the house was so still because he was trying to keep the warmth inside, not that it was working, and coming outside might have been a stark contrast. What he didn't think about was that he couldn't look up, that there might not have been a physical reason, rather an emotional one. Anyway it had taken so long because he had to be careful if he wasn't looking up, he had to avoid bumping into things. He stopped and listened to make sure if there was any traffic coming. As he was looking down, he saw a drop fall from his nose and disappear into the wet floor. If he looked away, he wouldn't be able to determine where the drop had fallen, so while he was thinking about where the drop had come from, he kept his eyes firmly on the exact spot where it had disappeared. Then another fell, and another. They didn't seem to contribute to the floor, only disintegrate into nothing.

He wasn't taking any deep breaths, he wasn't squinting, he wasn't covering his face, he wasn't clenching his teeth, or frowning, or feel like he was yawning or sighing; he felt quite ordinary, but he was definitely crying. It had been so long that he couldn't really hold it in. At that moment he realized that all the symptoms he thought he should be feeling were restraints on tears, they were not, as he had previously thought, in aid of them, or redundant even. But wasn't crying meant to be painful? Why wasn't he hurting, for himself or that jacket? Had he lost all feeling? What kind of emotions was he supposed to have?

Chapter *12*

'Hello. Hello Cherry, is that you?' He asked.

'No!' came a voice eventually, 'I don't know if she's in, I'll check her room. Wait a second.' The voice was disinterested, and obviously doing something as well as speaking on the phone that was distracting them, reluctance.

'Thanks.' Not that he meant it. It had taken him a lot of time to pluck up enough courage to call Cherry. He had tried to talk to others, but their reply, if any came at all, was not really satisfying. It felt like he had asked a lot of people about the letter he had received from April, actually he had taken so long and there were such gaps of indecisiveness that much time had passed in which it felt like he had called a lot of people. Maybe he hadn't got the answer he was looking for because he couldn't ask the right questions, it's difficult to ask what to do, to admit defeat. What made it seem like he had called so many people was that he had exhausted all the people he could possibly think of who might help. The voice never returned.

No doubt Cherry knew exactly what he was going to say to her and had already decided that she would be wasting her time talking to him. He was being optimistic calling Cherry, but he held on to the silent phone for a while hoping that her voice would acknowledge, it was either that he was optimistic or that he didn't really have anything else to do other than sit on the couch and wait. Nothing but wait, he had taken it upon himself to let the time pass as though it was the most noble, yet inconvenient task he could possibly undertake, a rewarding task, but one he would hate performing.

'Hi,' came Cherry's voice.

'Hi.' Maybe by copying her he thought that he would sound as well as she did, although that might defeat the object of his call. The truth was, now that Cherry's voice had turned up, he didn't really know what to say or ask. It was quite comforting to know that she was listening.

'What do you want?' asked Cherry in a sympathetic tone. Cherry was not the kind of person that would be dismissive straight away, maybe that was why he hadn't called her first, and left her until last, as a kind of last resort.

What she said sounded like she new exactly what he had called for. He waited a while, he forgot about the letter and just held the phone, it was quite like holding on to Cherry, although he dreaded that she might put the phone down, escaped from his grasp, at that moment he probably wouldn't have noticed. They used to have phone calls that were silent. It wasn't a waste of money for him, he felt that it was knowing that the person was there that made all the difference, like sitting in front of someone and looking in their eyes, yet not saying anything. Sure, discomfort was inevitable, but it separated the dishonest from the honest. At least it used to, but now he wasn't so sure anymore.

The distortion of the telephone wasn't as bad as the distortion of a television or radio, in fact it was comforting in a way, better than the dreaded tone of a hung-up deadness. The other might not be speaking yet they hadn't hung up either. He felt the pressure of needing to say something, but that just made him nervous and made it more difficult to think of something to say. That was when he realized that he had called because he was nervous. He was nervous about what might be wrong with him. He wanted to ask Cherry what the letter meant. What did it mean?

'Hi Cherry,' he said after calculating the finitude of Cherry's patience. He could hear a sigh of relief in the background and he knew that he deserved such a response, it wasn't a sarcastic thing that someone would do as an insult, it was because he was already asking a lot of Cherry by calling her and she was obviously in no mood for playing the silence game. 'How are you?' he said reluctantly. He didn't want to make it too obvious that there was something about himself that he wanted to speak about, but it was obvious that he didn't really care and that the whole conversation, if a conversation was going to take place, was going to be about him, as always.

'Yeah, you know, fine.' It was going to be difficult for her and she knew it, the words were coming out with great effort, like talking was something really difficult to do. And she wasn't going to tell him anything genuine anyway, only be polite, but she had earned the right to be able to do that because she had proved in the past that she was more than willing to do things for him, but felt that he hadn't appreciated what she had done for him. 'Listen, why don't you tell me why you called me?' She didn't have to say anything like that because it wasn't going to make any difference, but Cherry always took it on herself to say and ask the things that he wouldn't dare utter because he thought that they would sound ridiculous. When Cherry said them, though, they always sounded responsible.

'Well I got a letter from April.'

'And,' Cherry said at first and he thought that she was

saying she didn't care, 'what does it say?'

'I don't know... I... But... We... It's... It's sad, you know, that two people that want to be together... That have shared so much... It's like the letter that I got is from someone else that is trying to prevent us from being together.'

'I'm sorry,' said Cherry. She had understood more than was possible, but he didn't notice because he was in the habit, especially when it came to Cherry, of thinking that other people knew what he was thinking.

Maybe she was sorry, maybe she was afraid that if he didn't have anyone then he would come chasing after her and she didn't want to deal with him like that again. Whatever it was he did appreciate her offer of coming over and reading the letter to explain it to him. It wasn't that he needed someone to translate or anything like that, in fact he didn't know why he needed her to come over. He had an overwhelming need for someone to be with.

He lay on the couch and Cherry sat on the floor. He wondered how he looked, he knew that the position he was in was one that made him look ugly, he had seen himself similarly in a picture someone had taken of him. He knew that it pushed out his double chin and pulled in his chest that was small enough and really didn't need any reducing. There was something else that he felt uncomfortable about, the way he was lying, or the fact that he was lying at that time of day was a little lazy. And the more he thought about it the more he felt tired by the thought of doing things. He looked around the room and then looked at Cherry to see if she was looking at the mess in the same way he was.

'Are you alright?' asked Cherry.

He shrugged his shoulders. Cherry had startled him out of thinking that the house might not be as dirty as he thought it was, but something was making him annoyed with things, dust on surfaces, plants needing water, papers lying on tables, letters unread, dishes unwashed, carpets unvacuumed. There were just so many things to do and he didn't know which was most important to start with.

'You are lucky actually,' said Cherry, holding the letter up to catch his eye and his attention and to let him know that she was talking about the letter, 'she could have never told you these things.'

'What do you mean? Listen I never wanted to tell you that I was sad, that this fucking girl,' as soon as he said it he realized that, contrary to what he thought before, he actually felt extremely good mocking April and in a way he thought that April knew he was doing so, and in a way he was only saying what she wanted to hear, 'she would make me feel shit. I'm supposed to be feeling good because she lied to me, because I am stupid enough to be fooled into believing. How would that make you feel? Huh, how would it make you feel if someone told you they were in love with you and then said they were fucking joking? I can't believe it?'

Cherry was looking at him with disappointment in her eyes. 'No,' softly, then looking away.

That was when he realized that he had been raising his voice a little and saying things with malice, as though Cherry had been deceiving him and not April. That was when he realized that he was angry, that loneliness can make a person more angry than anything else can, maybe because it is the one emotion that can make one the most sad and because sadness so easily regresses into blame, and blame into anger. He didn't really know what she meant by what she said, but he was surprised. He was happy that she had come round, in a way it made him forget about April, or maybe it made him want to forget, either way the feeling of needing to do something, of not being able to do anything receded. It was one of the most horrible things, to feel unable to do simple things. Talking should be simple, he thought.

'I can't get over it,' his voice sounding as though it was searching for sympathy. 'I just don't get it, I remember her so well, you know, like her skin and her beautiful hair, it's like we had fallen asleep together and when I had woken up she was gone, just like that.' He felt like he wanted to say that he had woken up with nothing, but that felt like a bit extreme. After all he didn't want to sound redundant, in a way he wanted to show that he was strong and that he could deal with things, but it was a little obvious that Cherry coming over had already destroyed any possibility of being able to accomplish anything of the sort. He felt a kind of sickness that he would always get if he didn't know what to do, like he had experienced on many occasions with Cherry before, but this time it was a little different, this time he wouldn't gain anything, like he used to think he would, by blaming Cherry for anything that he was ashamed of. The problem was that it was difficult to think of anything else to do.

'No one ever lied to me before. Maybe they have, but I never found out. I never knew it'd make me feel so fucking abused.' He wanted to say that he felt pathetic because the lie took so much away from him, that he had realized that everything that he had, everything that gave him company, had been based on April's deception. He didn't know what was stopping him from saying it, he didn't think it was because it was too extreme, invisible in every sense, fear. He didn't want to look too deeply into why he was afraid, those areas were off bounds and made him angry even if he didn't notice, but it had something to do with looking weak.

'Listen, I really mean it; please don't take it like that; you are really lucky; she is being honest with you; most women wouldn't have told you anything; she is trying to show how much she does care for you, how much she doesn't want to hurt you. It's sweet that she is sharing this with you, trying to be honest, this letter...'

'Funny!'

'What?'

'Trying to be honest about being dishonest.'

'I know it sounds strange, but I can see what she's trying to say, can't you?'

'I hate the fact that you're right. I just find it difficult that it'd end like this, I thought honesty always made people feel better, with honesty there'd always be a winner, like the end would be good for me, I just couldn't see it any other way.'

It was strange having invited Cherry around for company, now that he had it he didn't want it. Nothing that had happened had been too bad to deal with emotionally, Cherry had been helpful, putting things into perspective and she had redeemed April instead of demonising her. He thought he had wanted April redeemed, he thought that would save everything, that he could still have confidence in someone that he had placed in such a powerful position, but it hadn't worked, and he didn't know what would.

Chapter *13*

He wanted to speak to himself, he didn't really know why because he always thought it was one of the most stupid things to do, he thought that there was no way that it would do people any good, he knew that it might help his grandmother, but with her it was okay because talking to oneself was what old people did, it was a sign of deterioration. What he wanted to say was that it wasn't true, that it didn't happen and he wanted people to hear it as well, but there was also part of him that didn't want them to hear, he wasn't really sure. He was sure, but his sureness only lasted for as long as his mind was focused, as soon as he started thinking about something else then his sureness switched to whatever else he was thinking about, so he was always sure, but not always about the same thing.

'I'm right!' slipped out, the words were quiet, almost hissing, not really audible, but far more real than when they were in his head.

When speaking, words are usually somewhat defined by the person who is listening, but what happens when no one is listening, when the speaker is alone, does the solitary individual entirely rule words, or does who they are thinking about have any impact on them? Does speaking need another to listen, or is the other already anticipated, or more precisely, does the other's desire to listen to something specific condition the speaker, or only this speaker?

He had noticed himself speaking, what he said might have come out unawares, but he was certainly surprised by hearing himself. He felt as though things reached a different point, when they were audible, not in volume, but in earnest. It was horrible.

Then the surprise went away and he thought about the way he had said things, so feebly like he was afraid to be heard, like he was afraid to hear himself. He almost hadn't heard himself, had he or hadn't he. He had never spoken to himself out loud before so he had nothing to judge it by, nothing to verify what speaking to oneself was like.

'I'm right,' slipped out again as if to make sure. But which was he confirming, that he had spoken out loud the first time, that he had heard himself, or that he was actually right?

He could explain to himself, silently, through thoughts or otherwise, through speaking to himself, that he was correct, that he was justified in what he had done the night before to Cherry, but then in no way would he be able to persuade himself that he hadn't committed anything at all. He wanted to believe that he hadn't, he was almost there at that point in fact, yet, the desire to be right prevented his arrival, or amnesia. Sometimes, when he had done something, and then slept on it, then he would wake up and have forgotten, for a while it was like he hadn't done it the day before, then he would remember, but then he felt a little insecurity as to whether it was real or not, perhaps because he didn't want to remember, perhaps because in a way he thought he could actually change the past by forgetting. Either way it was difficult to determine what, exactly he had done, he thought the difficulty was his own doing because he was actually afraid of what he had done, not that he could empathize with Cherry, but he was afraid to be himself. Hearing people confess something and then say that it was as if they were possessed by something was hard to believe, it was also hard for him to believe that he also felt like he had been someone else the night before, or at least that he had discovered that he was capable of something other than he thought he was, let alone believing what he had actually done.

Everything Cherry had said, every empathy, every sympathy, was incredibly easy to see from another direction, to see her words coming from a different direction, that is, with an ulterior motive, maybe an unfounded motive. Cherry didn't know how he was feeling, she couldn't possibly know what it felt like to have no friends, she had so many, everyone liked her, how could she be talking to him as if she felt sorry for the way he was feeling? How could she promise hope, when the last person he had hoped for had let him down? He had told Cherry about the letter he was writing to April, that he was writing about all her lies, and how he hoped to show her that lying wasn't going to get her anywhere. He had written that he thought it was April's fear of the truth that had driven them apart, not his desire to speak it. Cherry didn't disagree with him that he should say such things, but she didn't agree with him either, he couldn't remember what she had said, but he remembered feeling let down when she hadn't supported him, even questioned what he had written.

He and Cherry had spoken for hours the night before, words hadn't played any part in his cure, it was the fact that they were speaking at all, what was said mattered little. After a short while he had quite forgotten that when she was gone he wouldn't know what to do.

They had been sitting on the couch and Cherry had been

eating an orange, he remembered it so well because it was one of the most embarrassing incidences ever in his whole life. He had done something that he had vowed that he would never do. Embarrassing things were strange, they were kind of like trauma, but not exactly, they did traumatize, and that is where they converged, but embarrassment is different in that it isn't repressed in the same way as trauma. Traumatic experiences like grief, despair or unfulfilled desires are often so repressed as to be completely eradicated from memory until one doesn't even know of trauma, yet embarrassing situations are always remembered, but the pain surrounding, or even the anger, is what is traumatic.

Perhaps he had become carried away by the fact that they were speaking, he didn't know, but he was sure that he had flirted with Cherry in a way that he never thought he would dare. She had offered him a segment of her orange and he had accepted, when she was putting it in his mouth he reached just a little further with his lips until he touched her fingers. Noticing that she hadn't pulled back the next segment, he thought he might be a little more daring and actually sucked her fingers for just a second and then looked at her seductively, at least as seductively as he could. The third time he shut his eyes and sucked on the orange as though he was enjoying, and as though it was part of her body that he had in his mouth. Then he had kissed her, quite suddenly.

It lasted a few seconds and it was nice, but he pulled away and pretended he was overwhelmed by emotions. If he wondered how to make a face which expressed being drowned by emotions, then he couldn't possibly think of one and he had no idea how he looked, but he knew he'd succeeded. What he had been trying to express was that he didn't really know if what they had been doing was right, morally, emotionally, even physically as though the emotions might be taking his breath out of him or making him dizzy, and his face was trying to say that he needed a minute to think about whether he was doing the right thing, to come up for air. Honestly he wanted to continue kissing, but he wanted to show that he had learnt some things and that he was emotionally responsible for himself, because he knew he hadn't been in the past, and for her, because he knew that she might be thinking about how she would feel after everything, if anything actually happened.

Noticing how strange it was when things that he didn't want to think about were so hard to shake, like a tune that gets caught and one has to play, without wanting to, continuously, until it is lost when least expected and its absence isn't noticed.

He had looked at Cherry again and then tried to kiss her a second time, but she refused. Her refusal might have sent him into a frenzy, but he could remember that dismissal so it wasn't the most traumatizing. Because she had refused, he felt he had somehow lost everything, not only what he thought he had learnt or at least wanted to show and pretend he had learnt, but also Cherry herself. Her unwillingness, although it was hard to admit the next morning, had attracted him even more, unlike his wishes for her to be attracted to his unwillingness. Cherry could see through all of it, he couldn't even deceive her. How he came to the point of being angry with Cherry he couldn't recall, someone else might have taken her word and left her alone, but that would have meant being alone, if she was alone then he certainly was as well. The criticism that was coming out of his mouth wasn't really related to the event, but it was too late, he had shown his anger and he was too disgusted to apologise, he didn't feel like he had to, there was just no way. He knew that Cherry had perceived what had happened as a result of her refusal, perhaps that was what had made him feel like breaking something. He tried, in vain, to explain that wasn't the case, to break her stubbornness. It made him so frustrated that she could not understand him, that she could be so blind, so ignorant, raising his voice according to how much she disputed what he was saying. He told her that was her problem, that she was so superficial, that she could never be wrong. She said how many people agreed with her, and he told her, in as horrid way as possible, how many people she had slept with, and that they were all the people she had manipulated into agreeing with her. He told her that he didn't understand why she had friends if she was like that. He had said that they couldn't possibly be her friends, they were either as superficial as she or they were using her, that they weren't really friends. He was the only one that could be her friend because he was the only one that was honest to her, nobody else was because she wasn't honest to them. Everybody she knew was lying to her, because they all wanted to be like her, and if that wasn't the case, then he quoted things that they had said that would hurt Cherry if she heard them.

If ever she said something in her defence then he would quickly turn it around and throw it back at her, demanding that she was speaking defensively rather than honestly, asking her so as to make her agree with him. What he had said, at first, made her cry and then stop, attack him, be reluctant, be quiet, and laugh as though she was trying to show the stupidity of what he was saying.

He had said much more, but he started to feel sick when he remembered that he had thrown a glass of water over her when she refused to move, she had said that she wouldn't leave the house because she was still in the contract, she couldn't believe that he was throwing her out because she had done so much for him and he didn't realize it, after all, she had left for him. He couldn't believe it when he heard her saying that she had moved for him, he attacked her for pretending to be so caring and then using her responsibility to manipulate him. He knew that she was right, that she had made the move for him, but she couldn't now be using it against him, he said to Cherry that she should stop pretending to do things for other people and start doing things because she wanted to and not expect people to do things in return.

As soon as he had said something, he thought of what next to say and the criticism continued in a torrential downpour. Cherry tried to defend herself, but perhaps she saw the pointlessness of what was happening far earlier than he did, or maybe she was just stubborn, slowly she became more silent and more hidden behind cushions. In a way it made him feel like he had made his point and she was agreeing with him, but it also made him feel like she didn't care and that was what made him feel the worst. She should stop expecting so much of him, he said, she should stop thinking that he is so strong when he wasn't, he didn't really want to say that he was weak, but it was perfect in that it might have made her think that she had been abusing his weakness. Then he started to say how little she cared for him, how little of a friend she was, he remembered that he had said things about her not having friends, and he tied that into her way of mistreating friends, of him.

Cherry became really upset when he said that she didn't care about him. She said that was why she didn't sleep with him anymore, because she did realize that was a kind of usage, an abuse. She did care, that was why she had come round to listen to what he wanted to say, to try to help him. He just said that she came around to make him feel bad, worse.

The argument did fluctuate, it did turn, at points, into a sympathetic conversation. At one point he had told her that he needed help. That everyone, including her was against him, they might have been strong words, but they were going to catch her attention. That was when Cherry said she couldn't help him, that he should find professional help. He looked at her in agreement, but later said that she was only trying to hurt him when she said things like that, she accused him of being deluded and ignorant and traumatised. He wanted, in a way, to be like that, to be beyond help from any friend or relative, but at the same time he resented Cherry saying so, she was the one who was devious and corrupt and cunning and manipulative, how dare she!

Wanting to be someone else, like Cherry, but putting her down because of the impossibility, accusing her of committing everything that he knew he was doing, making her like him instead. He didn't want to be as pathetic as everything he had said. His words were pathetic, that's what they made her feel, that was their intention, but they were also, in themselves, so utterly pathetic that they made him feel that way by uttering them.

As he sat on the couch listening to himself, he realized that he had no one. No one to speak to. Did it matter? Gran didn't speak to anyone, at least hardly ever, that's what she said. But Gran was different, everyone she had known had died, Margaret was her last real friend. She could be felt sorry for because she hadn't pushed anyone away, she was likable, it wasn't her fault that she had no one, in fact it was partially his. Not only was he responsible for his own solidarity, but he was also accountable for his grandmother's. She went weeks without speaking to anyone she knew, maybe the gas man or a salesman or two, but then again so did he speak to them. He couldn't even go a few days without feeling sorry for himself. Gran never complained to him that she was lonely, but on his first encounter he had to tell her. Normally he would have been reluctant to tell her anything of the sort, they had so many secrets from each other, he couldn't tell her so many things for fear of hurting her feelings. When he put the phone down, he tried to imagine what she might be thinking of him, was she really concerned, or hadn't she taken him seriously at all, had she even hidden her will to accuse him of redundancy? He resented that he would never find out. She had told him to keep busy after he had said that he felt a little depressed, not that he felt justified. It was like saying he felt pain to someone that was dying, and then he felt stupid for using such an unhelpful, malicious comparison. It seemed that he couldn't really say anything to her, the words came out muffled and abrupt and he made a little laugh to hide what he really felt. But what exactly was she going to do? His grandmother told him to keep busy, that would keep his mind off things, whatever she thought was on his mind anyway, he knew she had some idea and he agreed with her, that was what he was going to do, keep busy.

'I'll try.'

Afterwards he thought he had sounded feeble, but if he was to have sounded optimistic and encouraged then he wouldn't sound serious about his feelings, it would be giving the wrong message. So, in a way he was saying what he felt, just in a very different language. What he was doing was what he said he would do while he was away, to express his emotions, instead of trying to look at them rationally and disguise them or pretend that they didn't exist. Express to the fullest capacity. Didn't Cherry do that?

Busy was exactly what he couldn't do. Nothing but struggle; he could think about doing things, then he would think about the next thing that needed doing and the next, and one took precedence over the other, all took precedence.

Eating, the preparation became so fast, the food that he made didn't represent someone that cared little for themselves, but because it was prepared so quickly, it was difficult to tell if he was actually taking care of himself. Cooking was one of the things he noticed the most, people with problems always had problems with food, at least everyone he knew. How could he sit at a table with no one and eat slowly and enjoy the food? He had thought about it and it hadn't seemed like such a bad idea, but that didn't mean that he was going to do it. The television became important. The programs were educational, all of them, but there weren't enough channels. He ate quickly and at the same time skipped through the channels so quickly that someone might be mistaken and think that he was watching all of them, often it did feel like he was both watching all the channels and that someone was watching him watching television. It was to become one of the most difficult experiences to cope with, having another's company, never being able to escape it, allow it to criticize and reduce everything he did, hate it, but want it because of lack of company. The kind of sharing that he was experiencing brought both solitude and companionship, he had to believe in it to survive, yet allow it to discipline and order him as though it eliminated all personal liberty. Didn't everyone have a partner like that?

Chapter *14*

A house is safe and friendly. Homely, some people might use the term to designate something secure and cozy. The home is somewhere that people can't see in and the outside world goes by without having any effect on the inside. Neither can the people inside see in, at least he felt he couldn't. Although there is only a thin sheet of glass separating the two at places, they feel a world apart. It is possible to stay inside for weeks, but the longer one stays inside the harder it becomes to emerge into the light. The air inside is still and warm, after long enough the body becomes the same temperature as the house, the eyes become accustomed and adjust to excrete just the right amount of fluid. But then, on contact, the outside is so noticeable, it even hurts, the eyes become dry and it is impossible to focus on anything for too long without a sudden tearing.

If one stays inside, one might not be able to exactly forget that there actually exists a space beyond the boundaries of brick or concrete that keep the warmth in and the cold out, but, in a way, forgetting is what it feels like. The will to meet people is forgotten, along with the will to see anything new, to keep up with culture, as if it really changes anyway. But what is most notably remembered is that everything might pass, continue, and forget, forget the insiders. Not, should be added, as though it was trying intentionally to accomplish eradication, no, that would donate a certain importance which he felt as though he would never deserve. He didn't think that people were exactly opposed to him, against him, that wasn't what brought the anxiety. Things, relevant or not, didn't become slow, so as to occupy and fill the time, instead everything was a rush or didn't happen at all. On many occasions he would put off going to the lavatory for as long as possible as though the television programme or the window was important, then he would leap up the stairs and not bother washing his hands afterwards.

Someone came around at one point, he thought that they came to collect the last of Cherry's things, it seemed the most appropriate reason for him finding out, his memory could have been failing him, but there weren't any other reasons for anyone to come around. He certainly hadn't invited anyone, didn't expect anyone, didn't even have much enthusiasm to open the door. He hated the people that disturbed him, and he had to get up with his head which was so heavy, if only he could have left it with it's unshaven face and uncut hair which he thought looked awful, and speak to whoever it was that was selling him religion and the kingdom of God. Cherry once said to him when his shoulders were uncomfortably stiff, that shoulders were like wings, at least the closest thing humans had to the point at which wings would meet the body and wings were what gave animals freedom, psychically, she was saying, shoulders, when tense, designate that the individual feels they are personally infringed. The tenser the shoulders the more unable, psychically, the person felt. He wondered what that should mean to him now that it was so difficult for him to move anything, arms, shoulders, legs, head, everything.

'Tell them to go away.'

It wasn't that they were wrong, quite the opposite, he was, not that they would persuade him to join them, but they would say that so much needed to be done, that it would be a difficult journey, but those who strove, who believed, who worked would inherit peace. It sounded tempting, but he was never going to be able to ask for any kind of forgiveness. There was no way he could ask anyone who came to the door, they didn't know what he had done, or hadn't done.

Would they listen? Did they ever listen? Didn't they hear him tell them to go away? Or did he just think about telling them to fuck off and politely listen to what they had to say, while they didn't allow him to interrupt even though he tried so frequently? Did he tell them how he was feeling and they hadn't taken any notice as though it was a job that they were doing and wanted to finish as soon as possible, not too dissimilar to the way he did things, except what he did at home was not a job, although it felt exactly the same? Those people that came to the door were employed, they had their work cut out for them searching for forgiveness, it was honourable, apologising, even though he knew they didn't feel guilty, that was what distinguished them. If only there was honour in apologising to everyone, just so that they might acknowledge him, not that he had done anything wrong, but because he hadn't done anything at all, no letter writing, no telephoning, no appreciating, not even attacking. It's no use apologising for nothing at all and then expecting someone to say that it was all alright, no harm done. Nothing done.

They had come to remove the last of Cherry's items and on their brief visit they said that Mario had died. He was curious to know how and they said that he had committed suicide, the details of which they were not sure of because it was second hand knowledge.

He shut the door behind them and he felt like he had missed his opportunity to gain some sympathy from someone. Did they not know what had happened between him and Mario, is that why they hadn't asked any questions, only speaking of Mario's death as though it would be embarrassing for them to come in and leave without saying something? Perhaps they didn't think that he and Mario had anything in relation? Maybe they didn't? Maybe he had been making it all up and actually he was just going to be another of Mario's sexual partners? Maybe he hadn't meant anything to Mario and sympathy was exaggerated? Maybe he shouldn't be feeling guilty, or sad, or somehow responsible in any way, that might be giving himself too much status?

Whatever he should be doing or feeling he decided to keep it a little secret of his own and assume that no one knew what had happened that strange night that seemed so long ago, but which now came back to haunt him. He could, in a way, make himself feel more important, like it was a matter of the strictest importance that it be kept a secret.

He sat down after standing in front of the door that he had held open and then closed for the brief visitor who could have been nice if they new something, but didn't make apparent if they did or not. He had felt the breeze, eventually, coming from the cracks around the door, which he had become sure was the same thing as the cold white light that didn't do much to warm or lighten the atmosphere, it might have been warmer to close the curtains which were orange and might have lightened the rooms, but he felt that they held too much of the smoke inside; he hated to see the smoke, suspended in mid air, almost solid, and he couldn't help wave it around a little as though it would make a difference. How he was disgusted by the people that he had seen in the launderette, which he never attended any longer, who had yellow moustaches and smoked the cheapest cigarettes wherever they were, around their children, in the launderette, walking along the street. Wasn't smoking a kind of social event that didn't need to be done while walking from place to place? The pure habit of it, the unenjoyment of it, the way it was so bound with poverty, disgusting. Yet, there he sat in front of the television, only moving when a certain part of the body became uncomfortable until, finally, he lay horizontal, smoking, and looking at the disgusting thin lines of blue-grey clouds. It was nice to inhale if one didn't think about those people, but as soon as one exhaled then it becomes impossible not to think about them in their houses with their children and their faces covered with acne and wearing cheap sports clothes like he had done a few years ago, overweight, pale, unhealthy, aggressive, uncaring. He felt different to them, not better just different, perhaps weaker, but he thought that was because he had seen that people could do better and compared himself.

He had been told about Mario's importance, not especially to him in particular, but Mario's importance to everyone. Over the days he thought about why Mario had committed suicide, what might have prompted him, but he couldn't think why, surely Mario had more friends than he had. Couldn't Mario get what he wanted, not that he felt as though he knew what Mario wanted, but he just guessed, or maybe the death was more important than that? He began to compare his life with Mario's, asking himself whether he had as much or as little as Mario had, whether he deserved to live more than Mario did, why people hadn't cared about Mario until his death, why they weren't thinking about him either. Had the suicide made Mario more important, or had it made him seem morbid and kinkier then before, or was it too late to become important? Maybe he hadn't done it for any of those reasons, maybe the decision to commit was far beyond anything he could comprehend, maybe he couldn't even possibly begin to understand, maybe no one could. Maybe no one cared and would never really, about any suicide. Maybe Mario's death donated, designated importance and made people talk about him, even if what they were saying was bad, at least it was something, it gave Mario a story.

He knew he didn't really have a story to tell, everything he said he felt was an exaggeration, or was stolen from someone less cunning. He hadn't anything which distinguished his individuality from anyone else's. All he had were experiences which he had time to scrutinize, criticize. Experiences which he could remember as though he was reading from a dear diary, that he would never have managed to keep up to date, or even start. Anyway, could words possibly be who he was? If only someone could explain to him why he couldn't live up to his, as yet, unjustified ideals, but no one was available. Perhaps he would only manage to justify them when he had lived them. How he wanted to tell a story, but he thought he needed someone to listen so he never did. He never believed in the stories that he told, that he thought he might one day tell, that he exaggerated, in fact he couldn't really think of any, not ones that people would take any notice of, they had to be enormous fabrications that were far out of his reach, and that was why he never tried.

Many times while going stale on the couch, he returned to thoughts of his criticism that so many had been hurt by, and he realized that he only had the ability to see and criticize what he thought wrong, which was not much of an ability at all. He wondered why he bothered for he had no means to compare the wrongs, his or anyone else's, with the unknown rights. He tried to justify his contradictions by inventing a victim, he tried to formulate an unavoidable consequence for himself, but he proposed an absolute and a truth which he couldn't ever dream of achieving. He thought he could become a victim of his own confusion now that he attested not to possess a simple reason of consequence by which to make his decisions, this he said, made his life impossible. But, the truth was that he found a simplicity in being absolutely selfish in his actions. Wanting to be nothing, he thought, must be the solution, but it would always be selfish, and that was exactly what he was. It didn't mean that he could accept that he was nothing.

After some time he thought that he might really have problems, not psychotic or schizophrenic, but more common ones, such as depression, or maybe lack of motivation was a mental health illness. After all he hated the idea of going out, but maybe hate was just a disguise for the fear of being seen, maybe going out would be a kind of confrontation with the necessities of life, to accept some kind of existence. Wasn't that what Cherry had said, that he needed professional help? How often when he had been out before had he become paranoid about something, how often did he think he had forgotten something, how often did he need to check that he had his keys? How worried was he that he might be beaten up? The more he thought about it the more it made sense, but he also became afraid, how exactly was he going to convince anyone as to the reality of these problems, does anyone with such problems actually know about them? What position would that put him in? Was it possible for him to be conscious of delusions from which he suffered, if he said that he was deluded would he really know from what he was suffering? If so would it be possible to create a distance so as not to be affected, or would he be able to persuade someone for unconditional sympathy? Unconditional it would have to be because of all the abuse he would hurl at them, after all, abuse would be necessary for their sympathy, but it would also mean that he would never be a better person than the kind he so dreaded being, and which he was trying so hard to persuade himself he wasn't. Perhaps he couldn't create a distance and he would really become what he was trying not to because he may see his problems, but he was so far from achieving any kind of acceptance. But he was so adamant that he could perform moral judgments and this complicated matters, because he thought that he shouldn't be able to if he was suffering from delusions which he could only suppose he had. Suppositions which he wished to rebel against at the same time as embracing. He found such a thin line between being able to help oneself, assuming that something was wrong might be the whole problem in the first place, and relying on someone else for help and comfort as an underlying problem. How was he going to decide?

Did his will to rebel, affirm an alternative, a life without being possessed by such a personality? He found it impossible to define and offer his individuality to anyone as he said he had been doing to everyone, but he couldn't have been because things would never have turned out as such if he had.

It was possible for him to explain periods of his past to himself and thus to decipher why he performed like he did. What difference would it make? He couldn't always manage to, and if he did it was always a solution only for other people, it didn't mean that he had to take his own advice or criticism. He wondered if he was his past, if he was all those horrible experiences he could remember. He wondered if other people felt about their pasts as he did. Would he ever be able to be spontaneous, changing things, doing something new and breaking the old destructive habit? The idea seemed impossible, how could he accomplish what he had never done before, how could he know what to do? Wasn't spontaneity the action of innocence which he had no part of? If he ever tried to tell someone else then his speech slowed, he was ashamed of what he thought and sad that he was ashamed.

A solution did appear shortly, it was to start admitting

things to others, as in a confessional, but before he got to the point of actually beginning, he thought that he would only admit his comparisons and judgments to others in order to appear happy. So he never really tried because he thought he might really finish with nothing. If he was his past then he was repeating himself in an inescapably comfortable manner, not realizing that his method of creating the order by repeating his trauma was in itself traumatizing. It was destructive as well as restorative.

The story that he thought Mario had might have been one that he needed in order to commit suicide, it might be something which justified it, a story might allow him the courage, it also might give him company in the same way it had Mario. He didn't want to die alone, he hated being in the house alone as it was, being without someone to love, maybe he didn't need them to love him as long as he could love them. At the same time he couldn't do it because of what others might think, even if an attempt would make them look, what would his grandmother think, what about his mother.

Part of him wished he could just slip away, even if he might be doing that already, he wished he could slip away and everyone would continue with their lives and he wouldn't have to, not as though they didn't care, but as though he didn't exist at all. In a way that was how he felt, like nothing, and he still couldn't do it, he was beginning to feel unworthy.

At least Mario might have had real problems and people could imagine, sympathize even with what might have gone wrong, or thought about possibilities of things that might have gone wrong. But they were never going to do that for him, nothing was that bad for him, he had it all and he was fucking it all up, fucking things up was no justification for suicide.

Nothing good could be found inside himself, summoned, that made him feel bad, awful, but at the same time it was a step towards being definite about something. All he needed was to find bad things. The only one he could find was unworthiness, he had been dishonourable. He wasn't worthy of committing suicide, of giving shit to anyone who tried to help him, in a way it would have been part of rehabilitation, had he needed it, but he didn't. He wasn't worthy of being spoken to, of pretending to have problems that others might need to listen to, he wasn't worthy of telling them. How could he be when he couldn't really admit that he had problems to himself?

He knew someone once, in his school, who he had found hanging by his neck from a tree. He remembered that he had run as fast as he could, saying to himself that they should not do it, after someone else had told him something about a rope and Andrew at the swing that they had all been using. But there were two in the school, one at each opposite end of the grounds which were very large. He didn't know which one they meant and had run to the closest one, to find that Andrew wasn't there, he then ran to the other expecting to find Andrew threatening to hang himself, he was sure of it. When he arrived, he was shocked to find that he was too late and somehow never forgave himself that if he had run to the right swing then he might have saved Andrew.

Andrew was wearing a stripey jumper and it was a strange sight, like a prisoner that couldn't take the time any longer. He was told to hold him as high as he could. Andrew was so heavy and he struggled with all his strength. It was necessary so that everything would be alright. He was saying what an idiot Andrew had been while they tried to cut him loose, but Andrew never heard him.

Ever since then he had thought about it as an honourable death, in fact straight afterwards he lay on his bed with clean clothes, that he had changed into for reasons he couldn't remember, and not really been able to feel that Andrew had done something selfish or taken the easy way out, escaped, where to? As though more than sympathy was deserved. He thought that Andrew had confronted everything that there was to confront, not exactly that Andrew was courageous, but that he had seen things that others never would be able to see. He hated when, years later, people talked about it and used the memory as though it was something excitingly tragic. Nobody could say anything about Andrew's death because they didn't know what they were talking about. Some people said that they still didn't know if it was suicide or an accident, but he had seen things, and he wasn't afraid to say it was suicide. He had to pay his respects to Andrew, not that he thought he was such a great person when he was alive, to the contrary he had always teased and persuaded him, but he had to respect what he had done, however strange it might sound to anyone, it never did because he never told anyone. The respect he felt for Andrew was one that reminded him of soldiers, of the picture in Margaret's room, of his Grandad, everything he was not worthy of. In a way he thought that Andrew had given his life for something like the soldier in Margaret's picture, like his Grandad, they didn't think about selfish things, they had given or taken lives in a respectful way that no one now could understand. It was an innocent way, and an innocent could never use escapism, not like he could. Even if he could, no one else would see it that way. He wasn't worthy of the honour and, besides, now he felt as though he would just be imitating like everything else he had done in his life, nothing was worse than that, he couldn't do anything for himself.

For days he thought the same things over, he thought time

would move them on, that he might develop or grow out of the routine, that he would come up with some great thought that would change his life somehow, but it never came. And he waited, he didn't really know what for, he didn't even know that he was waiting, it was just a term that he thought of later, it didn't make the thoughts, the dirt, his pathetic incapability any easier, perhaps worse, waiting only allowed them to take a stronger hold. But no one would believe that he was a suffering individual, that was stupid, completely stupid, what they would think was how horrid he was, treating them like shit all the time, pretending to be better. Couldn't that be a problem in itself, thinking that other people weren't helping him at all, not being able to respect them? But he did, at least he thought so, more than anyone, he was the only one that really knew what friendship was about. Wasn't he supposed to learn from what people said to him, or was he supposed to become angrier and demand they were ignorant?

'I haven't spoken to you,' he wrote to April one day, *'for what seems like such a long time, in terms of what I would like to say to you and how confused I am. I'm sure we are both hurting and hiding as much as each other. I wish I could just say to myself that it was enough, that I suffered enough, and just separate and distance myself from this whole situation. In fact I do say it to myself, with the whole*

backing of my ideals, but it works, and I can't. What I am saying is that I forgive you. I am so sad that you felt you needed to lie to me and so often. I guess you had to carry on after you began. Now you are so deep that you don't know what to do except to carry on and continue deceiving because, by this time, you will hurt people so much if you do anything else. Don't you realize that so much of your life is fake, that you can't be close to the people you want to be closest to, to the people you have deluded yourself into thinking you are closest to? How can they be? They are ignorant of so much. They don't love you, they love the other person that you have created. I'm sure they would still love the real April as long as you gave them a chance. It hurts me to see this happening to you. You are the only one losing here! You are so selfish because you don't want to let other people decide things for themselves, you decide for them. All because what they decide might hurt you, might be different to what you decided, to what you want...'

He never finished the letter, what he wanted to do was explain so much that he thought he understood, but it became too complicated. How could he ever explain anything to her? He only wanted to say that he forgave her, he really thought that she didn't want to be with him because she had hurt him, and that if he forgave her then she would be with him. He never sent it, he couldn't, just couldn't.

'Dearest April,' he wrote, *'I tried to work out who I am, to pressure my convention. I'm afraid of whom I am, I'm afraid of people knowing my age. I fear maturity. My own. I run as fast as I can, putting my eyes where only my thoughts can see. Occasionally falling over my suppression. Retention. Fleeing my own embarrassment. Spelling my incorrectness. Looking away when all was visible, when all could see. When seeing is all that can be.*

'Normally I am always searching for victimization that I can blame for superficiality. With so many values to depend on, a will to disagree, to perpetuate my comfort, what remains? Am I my age, my every dependency?

'I wrote this to you because I am not afraid of sharing myself with you. Because I am not all these. They are what I try to be. If I am anything more than my pity for myself then I am my love for you. And if that's all I am then I am also happiness.'

He thought that saying he loved her would be the right thing, instead of being angry; showing he was the same as her, in the same position.

He hated going to bed every night, he did always have terrible dreams, that wasn't something that he had made up, it wasn't a lie like everything else that he wouldn't ever be able to escape because he had forged so much of his life. He hated going to bed also because he dreaded waking up and wondering what to do with the day. So he spent so little time actually sleeping, most of the time he spent laying down, thinking, but he never thought about anything unless he knew he could always quickly move onto the next subject. He didn't want to sleep, but he never wanted to get up either, it was a strange relationship. No one enjoys watching television, no one wants to sit on the couch all day and think that they can't do anything, that everything is too difficult for them and only them. How could he have fallen into the trap, how could he have brought all on to himself? Did he really want to feel bad? Couldn't he be happy for anyone? That was the problem, everything that he didn't do was awful, he couldn't enjoy anything he didn't have a part of, and now that he wasn't doing anything, everything became appalling. For weeks he watched all monstrosities out through the window, all horridness which slowly engulfed his room and thoughts more and more, until he could think of nothing else but the plan of how he was going to raise himself, by whatever means, above it all. The room was getting darker, it was being penetrated by everything he hated outside, it wasn't his imagination, it was because his hate for his room developed. But there wasn't anywhere else to go, he would always take whatever it was that made him resent wherever he went. He would never be able to leave his pathetic nature, his inability, he would always at some point or another have to allow it to catch up with him, when he had to tell someone the truth, when he was cornered without a planned lie.

What was he going to say when he arrived? He didn't exactly remember where the GP was, the last time he went was so long ago, to pick up a doctor's certificate for Cherry saying that she didn't have to go to work.

It was cold outside, almost snowing, not knowing whether it was going to or not, not knowing weather. If it was snowing then he could have said that he had to stay in, or at least when he arrived it would give him a solemn, practically homeless, unshaven, hopeless appearance. Did he need it to lend a seriousness to his begging for help? After all he was doing the last thing on the list of possibilities, was that not good enough, bad enough? Nobody wanted to go to the doctor, a stranger, that was just like everyone else, and say that they couldn't cope. Or was he begging prematurely? Did he have any real problems? If he didn't, wouldn't they slowly manifest themselves until it might be too late? Maybe he was doing the responsible thing and trying to catch whatever it was early enough, maybe that put him one step in front of anyone else, gave him an edge, but if he had an edge then he wouldn't have to worry. Did he have to worry? Of course he did, at least that was what he had decided to tell the doctor, after all, the problem didn't have to matter, it could be how much someone worried about it. Chronic anxiety. How did that categorize him? Hopefully only enough to get some antidepressants, he wasn't willing to go much further, he didn't want to be an inpatient or anything. Therapy perhaps, then at least if he wasn't getting any better it would be someone's fault.

But when he was thinking and he had only himself to confront did he really have anything to be concerned about. There were certain things which were continually recurring. And he remembered the time of his first sexual experience, since when he couldn't ever have sex without remembering that moment, it wasn't such a bad memory, but it was possible to make it sound horrific if he really wanted. Besides, it was what put him off sleeping with Mario. Could it even really be bad and because he was so ignorant he wasn't noticing the pain, repressing it? If he heard someone telling him the same story, he would think that they should at least be slightly disturbed.

The man is old, perhaps four times his age. The man is lying there in bed, ill, drinking, it's in a cup, saying that it is a remedy of some sort, like tea, but there is alcohol in it. He can tell. Besides it's no secret, everybody knows an alcoholic, drinking all the time. He wants to drink as well, everyone he knows wants to drink. He remembers, he thinks, having some rum, he thought it was so cool, something he could tell everyone about, how much he had to drink, it was something that older people did. He was lying on the bed with the man and he said it was so hot. The man was so crude, able and strong. And he was always right about everything. He took off some of his clothes. It was silent except for the man's jokes, the man laughed so much and he laughed with him. The man made everything seem so straight forward. He knew that everything the man did or said was right and he believed him. It felt so good to be alone with him. He felt everything the man was saying was for him, alone. Answering all his questions and telling him everything he wanted to know. And giving him as much as he wanted to drink. He felt so free, he felt like the man, mature. It wasn't like being around friends of his age, he could be the man's friend. He knew the man was naked and he took off all his clothes. Around people his age he worried what he looked like, but not then. He wanted so much to show that he could do whatever the man could and he didn't want to be told that he was wrong. The man touched his dick. It was so small compared to the man's large fingers. The man played with it for a while, and never looked in his face, only at his dick. He felt it was something special between the two of them. He let the man do whatever he wanted. Then the man stopped and put it in his mouth, sucking on it really hard. He felt the scratching from the man's moustache on his belly. He couldn't remember if he said anything after that, or while the man was doing it. He wondered what it felt like for the man in his mouth. It felt warm. Nobody had ever touched his dick before. He had made it hard on his own, but no one else had. The man got up to go to the toilet and left him feeling really alone, but the man had made him feel really strong. He felt that he could give everything the man would want. The man must still want him. The toilet flushed and he quickly lay himself out. The man came back and smiled, looking at him for a while, he looked at himself, at his body. Then it all continued again, except the man wasn't so interested. His head hurt when he woke up the next morning. He didn't know how he had got to his own room, to his own bed, but he had. The man was still in the house, but he kept quiet so the man wouldn't hear or see him. He hid behind the door when the man passed. He didn't want his mother to know.

He remembers, he thinks, that's the problem, would it be better if it was untrue or true? Would it mean that he really had problems if it was true? He wished he had put up a fight, he had let it happen to him, even encouraged it, did it count then as a traumatic event. He would always be ashamed, he would never be able to tell anyone, ever. He wished that the fear of anyone finding out would disappear, but it never seemed to even diminish, slightly. The shame mostly came from thinking that he couldn't think the experience was abuse, or that it had damaged him because he could have avoided it, at least not provoked it. Did he have an excuse, could he say that because he was young he didn't know that it would affect him in such a dramatic way? Or, was he making up the effect? What was actually traumatic about the whole thing, that he remembered, that he was making too much out of it? He had even got himself into the situation that he was, without anyone to talk to, cold, resentful, look at the damage that he was doing to himself. He wished he had put up a fight, but persuaded himself, even though he thought otherwise, that it wouldn't have made the slightest difference. The hardest thing to admit was going to be that he hadn't said "no".

He would always remember the image of his body, lay out, it would never change, he would always have the body of a boy.

He couldn't tell that to the doctor though. How could he say that he had encouraged an older man to abuse him, was it even abuse? No, what he would do would be far cleverer, he would anticipate, like he had learnt to do as a child, what the doctor wanted to hear. He knew he could do it, he had to. He had done the same to Cherry, and he was going to do the same on the phone to the Samaritans, except he had never begun to look for the number.

Could other people deal with fears and anxieties, was he inferior? That was what he was thinking and it made him feel awful, he would have to damage everyone, everyone was to blame, but no one was, he knew that, but he wouldn't be able to help it, wasn't that enough? Making up problems might be a problem in itself.

But he didn't want to eventually have to go to a clinic, he had to balance stories so as not to fall in the wrong category. he knew what a clinic was like, he had seen them, the people, doing nothing, no one caring, they were places that people were supposed to care, but they were worse. No one could get better like that, in old, damp houses that were cold, with nothing to do but smoke. How he hated damp and stale smoke, home.

He hadn't been anywhere or done anything, he always made it appear as though he had done so much and been to so many countries, sure he had, but he was beginning to realize that it hadn't made him any different, he hadn't learnt anything. He couldn't even find a job, why couldn't he? He thought that it was because he was too afraid, he couldn't do anything, the best he could do was work in a supermarket. He said that working in a supermarket or a similar job was honourable work, but only to hide the fact that he couldn't do anything else, he hated the moments of telling people what he did, how little he learnt.

The doctor wasn't going to believe anything he said anyway, they were just going to laugh at him and send him home. Would he be able to recite all these things to someone that he didn't know? Would they be able to tolerate all the abuse that he had given to anyone that had tried to help? At most, the doctor was going to listen and suggest some sort of counselling, maybe that was all he needed, but it couldn't be, he hated so much, was there a therapy for hate? How could he have hated everyone that tried to help him, or didn't know that he was feeling like shit, he was feeling fine? He knew that to blame someone else was the wrong thing to do, it was out of the question, but it was bigger than him, and before he knew it he wanted to hit them. They were innocent, but they weren't, because they were just trying to make him feel inferior to them, less capable of dealing with emotions, patronizing him. All they did was pity, how many times he had thought of Cherry just fucking him out of pity? Why did she pity him so, because he was in love with her, because she knew he was, because he couldn't find anyone else? Even the sex he had was because he was crap. He thought, for a moment, he had started using the fact that he couldn't do anything to his advantage. He didn't need pity. Oh yes he did. He hated that need, he didn't want to need anything, why did he need people when everyone else could manage on their own, why could they all manage so much better than he could? The doctor wasn't going to believe until he did, but it was difficult to believe that one has problems, that's the last thing anyone wants to do, is capable of doing, accepting the affliction. Addiction to masochistic affliction.

As usual he had not put enough clothes on, it was terribly cold and he felt like he usually did, that he was going to catch a cold, he could feel the soar throat already coming on. He turned the corner into the street that led to the health centre. He was registered there, but he didn't know what the doctors name was, he'd forgotten. For a few minutes he wondered what exactly it was that he was going to do. Nothing was ever going to work, nothing at all, now that he really made an effort. It was closed. The clichés were true. They were no longer clichés, the clichés had died and become truths of transgression. The impossibility of admitting nothing, saying nothing is not, necessarily, admitting nothing. Is it worthwhile to be nothing more than a plague, of dismissal, of bonds which only justify by means of themselves; your own?

I.S.B.N.: 84-88423-128